# FOREWORD

I started filming *Lost Christmas* in Manchester in March 2011, after having just finished filming *Treasure Island* in Puerto Rico.

Filming the role of Long John Silver in *Treasure Island* and then, two weeks later, the role of Anthony in *Lost Christmas* was a challenging opportunity and a drastic weather change. But I'd spent years trying to get to get roles like these.

The film story and the book story of *Lost Christmas* are slightly different, but I hope they will give people the same overall feeling – that it's always good to hear a tale about a little magic at Christmas.

Anthony is a character who knows no fear. He can't feel fear as he has lost all his memory, and this gives him his magical quality. He knows he has a mission, but has no idea what that mission is. He keeps having visions that scare him but also rather intrigue him.

He wanders through our story with the innocence of a child and the knowledge of a god – a god who knows only the weird stuff. He also has a spiritual link with other people's lost things, but again he has no idea why.

In the end I think Anthony is the spirit of Christmas past and the spirit of Christmas future rolled into one.

Once upon a Christmas present . . .

*Eddie Izzard, November 2012*

# LOST CHRISTMAS

## DAVID LOGAN

Based on a screenplay by John Hay and David Logan

Quercus

*For Lisa, Joseph, Grace and Gabriel*

First published in 2011 by Quercus

This paperback edition published in 2012 by

Quercus
55 Baker Street
7th Floor, South Block
London
W1U 8EW

A CIP catalogue reference for this book is available
from the British Library

ISBN 978 1 78087 836 2

1 3 5 7 9 10 8 6 4 2

Printed and bound in Great Britain by Clays Ltd, St Ives plc.

# 1
# LAST CHRISTMAS

Goose woke to the distant sound of a dog barking. It wasn't much of a bark. More of a yip. A yip that belonged to a small dog. A puppy. And not so distant. Actually . . . close. Very close. In his house close.

He heard it again, pushed himself up on one elbow and listened. His wild, all-over-the-place hair stuck out all over the place. Goose had big, green, soulful eyes. Right now they made him look cute. A few years from now they'd be the sort of eyes that made girls go weak at the knees. His mum said that to him all the time, which made him cringe.

'Girls suck!' he would say, and he meant it. His mum would smile, that all-knowing smile grown-ups have that means I know something that you don't because you're only

1

ten. Goose hated that smile. He hated being patronized. Most of all he hated the fact that he suspected she was right; there was something he was missing. Things were so much simpler when he was nine, he thought.

The yipping had stopped. He tilted his head to listen. A sliver of white light caught his eye as it crept in through the gap at the top of his Man City F.C. curtains. They were pale blue and spotted with the old ship and Lancashire rose emblem. His dad refused to let him update to the later eagle and stars shield. He said that the rose and the ship on the Manchester Ship Canal represented the city. What did an eagle have to do with Manchester?

Goose was an avid supporter. His walls were plastered with posters: lots of City, naturally, and *Doctor Who*. There was Luke Skywalker, Han Solo and Princess Leia, Iron Man, Harry Potter and Thor. There was a stack of books and comics on his bedside table. Goose was a voracious reader. He loved books. He also loved films, football of course, swimming, dragons and computer games. He considered himself a bit of an all-rounder.

He couldn't hear anything now. Maybe he was wrong. Maybe he had imagined it. Maybe it was the end of a dream. That happened sometimes, in the few short seconds between dreaming and waking when the two states merged. Goose liked dreams. He liked the idea of dreams.

Once his mum had taken him to a lucid-dreaming

2

workshop. Goose had asked the man running the workshop a question he couldn't answer. The man was impressed. Especially as Goose was the only child in attendance and none of the adults had thought of any question half as interesting. The man had said that it was not possible to turn a light on or off in a dream. Goose had asked if it was possible to light a match in a dream. The man had thought about it, but in the end had to admit defeat. He just didn't know.

Goose's dad had sneered at the idea of lucid dreaming. He didn't believe in all that nonsense. No, that wasn't entirely true. His dad said he was 'a healthy sceptic' – whatever that was. He didn't believe in ghosts or UFOs or God, but he wasn't arrogant enough, his dad would say, to know for sure they didn't exist. He liked to keep an open mind about such things. That open mind didn't extend to astrology, which Goose was sure had to be based in science. It did end in '-ology' after all. But his dad said it was nonsense. How could six billion people be categorized by something as random as birth date? Auntie Alice, Dad's best friend Frank's wife, really believed in astrology, and when Uncle Frank and Auntie Alice came over for dinner Dad and Alice would invariably argue the rights and wrongs of astrology. Alice would say there's so much more to it than just birth date, and Dad would say that at best astrology could group people together in very general categories that didn't take into account environment, education or experience and therefore was about as much use as a chocolate teapot or shoes for fish.

Goose was wondering why that thought had chosen to pop into his mind at that particular moment when he heard another yip. It was definitely coming from inside the house.

He jumped out of bed to investigate, stepping straight on to a Lego model of Imperial AT-ST.

'OOWWW!' He fell back on the bed and rubbed the sole of his foot. He looked down at his bedroom floor, which was strewn with pieces of Lego and other toys. There was a whole bunch of Transformers and *Doctor Who* figures in and around a wooden castle in the middle of the room. Several versions of the Doctor had joined forces with Optimus Prime to battle three dragons and numerous knights. Evil knights of course, who had been possessed by the spirit of Seerg the Destructor (who had taken the form of a giant gorilla). Goose had been in the midst of the final battle last night; the future of the universe rested in his hands. It was a gargantuan responsibility that many a lesser individual would have shied away from, but not him. He was up to the challenge. He was Batman, he was Aragon, he was Captain James T. Kirk and he said *BRING. IT. ON.* But then his mum had made him go to bed.

Another yip from downstairs. Goose forgot all about the game and hurried to the door, being careful to step only on safe, clear patches of carpet. He pretended he was Indiana Jones as he approaches the idol at the beginning of *Raiders of the Lost Ark*, tiptoeing precisely. He reached the door and slipped out into the hallway.

Goose's real name of course wasn't Goose. It was an affectionate nickname that started at an early age and stuck. When he started to crawl, which according to his mum he did very early, he would invariably try to crawl away, to escape. When he matured into a toddler, he would toddle off at any opportunity. His parents couldn't take their eyes off him for a second. Once, when Goose was not quite two, they were at Manchester Airport, waiting to collect Frank, Alice and their daughter, Jemma, returning from two weeks in Tenerife. Goose's mum and dad turned their attention away from Goose's buggy for all of thirty seconds as they scanned the arrivals board to see if the plane had landed. In that time, Goose somehow managed to squirm out of the straps holding him in and wander away. When Mum turned back Goose had vanished into the hordes of holidaymakers. An exhaustive and frantic search of the airport followed, and eventually he was found sitting on a plane about to take off, destined for Greece. No one was quite sure how he had managed to avoid the airport's extensive security. The

*Manchester Evening News* had written a little article about his adventure, and his dad had joked that he had been a goose in a past life and was trying to fly south for winter. So even though he was christened Richard Michael Thornhill, he had answered to the name Goose for most of his life. And even now at the grand old age of ten, Goose rarely stayed in one place for very long. The world was big and he was hungry to see it all.

As Goose headed to the stairs, he could hear muffled voices coming from below. He passed his mum and dad's bedroom. The door was open and he could see the big bed was empty. The white duvet was turned down at both top corners and turned up at one bottom corner. Goose knew this was because Mum was always cold and Dad was always hot. They had a special duvet that was thicker on one side (Mum's) than the other. The bottom corner was turned up because Dad always slept with his feet exposed. Goose was the same. He loved those little similarities he noticed between himself and his parents.

As he trotted down the stairs, past a series of photographs of himself as an infant and three canvases that Mum had bought when he was little and made him walk across with paint-covered feet so his baby footprints walked down the wall, he could hear his parents' voices along with that of his nan. They had heard him coming and were

6

busily trying to hide something. Goose reached the bottom of the stairs and pushed open the door to the living room.

His mum, Linda, his dad, Paul, and his nan, Nan, turned to face him, shoulder to shoulder, forced closed-mouth smiles on their faces.

'Awright there, Sir Gooseby?' said his dad. Goose liked that nickname. Other times his dad called him 'sausage', which he really wished he wouldn't. 'What are you doing up so early?'

'What's going on? I heard barking.'

'Barking?' His mum was trying to sound casual. She wasn't good at it.

'Must've been outside,' said Dad.

Just then, there was another yip, and Goose could see a dog bouncing up and down excitedly behind his parents and his grandmother.

'Dad!' Goose came further into the room, weaving left and right, trying to get a better look at the animal.

'We were going to hide him till tomorrow,' explained his mum, 'but he doesn't seem to want to play along with that plan. Happy Christmas, sweetheart.'

And, with that, Mum, Dad and Nan stepped aside, revealing a small brown and white mongrel deeply engrossed in a satisfying scratch behind his ear. With an open mouth Goose looked down at the dog. The dog stopped what he

7

was doing and looked up at Goose. Their eyes met. And it was love at first sight.

Goose dropped to his knees in front of the dog, who bounded forward, paws up on Goose's chest, licking him manically, tail wagging back and forth two hundred times a minute.

'What is he?' asked Goose.

'He's a dog,' said Dad.

'No, I mean, what breed?'

'He's a bitsa.'

'A bitsa?'

'Bitsa this, bitsa that,' Dad smiled.

Goose groaned. He should've seen that one coming.

'What you going to call him, love?' asked Nan.

Goose pondered the question as the dog bounced around him in a circle of barely contained excitement, yipping and pausing now and again to lick or sniff his new master, or scratch himself. After a moment Goose gave up and shrugged. 'Don't know yet. I'll think of something.'

Paul crouched next to his son and his new pet. The puppy lay on his back submissively and Paul tickled the dog's belly. 'There's a good boy!' He smiled at Goose. 'He's had all his shots. Wanna take him out?'

The sides of Goose's mouth strained to encapsulate his grin. His entire body thrummed with total and absolute joy. He couldn't remember a time when he'd been happier.

He felt elation coursing through him, as if it was a physical thing: a thick luminescent liquid filling him up. Even his ears felt happy. At that precise moment, the phone rang and the smile faded from Goose's face. His mum went out into the hall to answer it. His dad looked at him, still smiling, and gave a small shake of his head.

'It's awright. I'm not on call,' he said.

Just as Goose was starting to smile again, Linda came back into the room. 'Paul, it's the station. Jamie's broken a finger, had to go to A&E.' The smile on Goose's face was only just starting to reignite. It went out like a candle in a storm. Paul frowned and looked apologetic, but there was nothing he could do. He mouthed the word 'sorry', but knew it didn't help.

Goose watched as his dad stood up and strode out into the hallway. Paul took the phone from his wife and listened.

Nearby Nan was making her way along the mantelpiece, turning all the Christmas cards upside down. Goose looked at her, but the strangeness of her actions didn't register with him. His mind was elsewhere. He looked back to the hallway just as his dad glanced back at him. Then Paul turned away and sighed. 'Yeah, okay, I'll be there as soon as I can,' Goose heard him say.

He looked down at his new puppy frolicking in front of him, rolling this way and that and then getting startled by his own tail. Something silver caught his eye and he saw a set of car keys sitting on the coffee table, at eye level, a mere arm's reach away. A dozen thoughts raced through Goose's head, all of them colliding into a jumble and not one of them making any more or less sense than any of the others. So, without thinking, his hand shot out and grabbed the keys. He pushed them under the cushion of the mauve Dralon-covered armchair behind him just as Paul came hurrying back in, clearly looking for something.

With the puppy still a non-stop ball of excitement before him, Goose watched as his dad picked up magazines from the coffee table and rooted around the mantel.

'You seen my keys anywhere, Goose?'

Goose shook his head as little as possible; somehow that made it less of a lie.

Paul stopped searching and looked at his watch. He cursed under his breath. Then he made a decision and called out: 'Linda, you're gonna have to drive me, love.'

A small barbed ball of anger lodged in Goose's throat. He clenched his lips tightly shut so he wouldn't say anything he'd regret. He breathed through his nostrils and let the bitterness mushroom inside him. *This always happens,* he thought. His dad was always working. It wasn't fair. Sometimes he hated his dad. He spoiled everything. He was so selfish.

Goose glanced down at the puppy, who had stopped spinning and was now watching Goose, his head cocked to one side as if he could tell something was wrong. It was almost as if he could read Goose's mind, and for a moment Goose felt ashamed of the thoughts he'd had. However, that didn't change the fact that his great plan had been foiled. He watched as his mum and dad left.

Paul and Linda climbed into Linda's green Ford Focus and drove away from the cul-de-sac where they lived. Linda was driving. She turned right at the end of the street. It was still early and the roads were mostly empty. They saw the occasional milk float or delivery truck. They drove in silence for a few minutes, but both were thinking the same thing.

'I'll make it up to him,' said Paul.

'He'll be fine. He's got Ronnie to distract him.'

'Ronnie?' Paul frowned. *Who's Ronnie?*

'Ronnie Barker. Thought it was a good name for the dog. What d'you think?' Linda smiled at her husband.

He grinned. Twelve years of marriage and they still made each other laugh.

'Little out of date for Goose, isn't it? He won't have the first clue who Ronnie Barker is.'

Linda indicated to turn left.

'You should take Langford Street,' said Paul. 'It's quicker.'

'It's not going to matter much at this time, is it?' It

irritated Linda when Paul tried to tell her what to do when she was driving. They'd never had an argument about it. Linda mostly just swallowed her irritation and carried on doing what she was planning to do in the first place. Women had been doing that for centuries. It's how most marriages survived. Paul's unconscious habit of pressing his right foot down when it was time to brake was also annoying, but, seeing as he wasn't even aware he was doing it, Linda had never said anything.

'I suppose not,' said Paul. He switched on the radio. 'Wonderful Christmastime' by Tom McRae was playing. 'Oh, I haven't heard this for ages.' Paul hummed along with the song, half a second slow as always. Linda smiled.

Then, out of the corner of her eye, she noticed something red. It was moving fast. Too fast for her to even turn her head. Too fast for her to form any words to say to her husband. About the same time, Paul saw it too. It was an LDV Convoy van. Red. The driver was a middle-aged man called Eric Cutty. A late night and an early start had got the better of him and he had drifted off to sleep just for a moment, his foot on the accelerator. The van shot out of the T-junction at speed. Eric jolted awake. He saw a tree ahead. He didn't have any time to react, but his mind calculated in a fraction of a second that he wouldn't hit the tree . . .

. . . because of the small green Ford Focus approaching from his left.

The van ploughed into the side of Linda's car. In the split second before impact, Paul stamped both feet down into the well of the passenger's side with as much force as he could muster. His unconscious was trying to brake, trying desperately to stop the car.

Linda did the same thing on the driver's side. The difference being that she was able to press down on the brake for real. It made no difference. The car was lifted up off the tarmac by the snub nose of the van. A kind of clarity settled in Linda's mind. She knew she was about to die and she wanted very much to kiss her little boy one more time.

'Goose . . .' she said, and then everything went black.

## 2

# THIS CHRISTMAS

Mick, the landlord of the Three Witches pub, had a great sense of humour. Or at least that's what he thought. He prided himself on his entertaining quiz nights. If they weren't rolling in the aisles, he wasn't satisfied. The problem was that Mick just wasn't funny. It wasn't the material, it was the delivery. Mick would steal jokes from the best. There's an old gag by the comedian Tommy Cooper that goes, 'Apparently, one in five people in the world is Chinese. And there are five people in my family, so it must be one of them. It's either my mum or my dad or my older brother Colin or my younger brother Ho-Chau-Chou. I think it's Colin!' The problem was that Mick would always forget to name the brothers, and then when no laughs were forthcoming for several long, excruciating seconds, he would remember his mistake and then try to explain that one brother was Chinese. Then he would remember it's saying the names that's the funny bit, but by then the joke was dead and Tommy Cooper was cringing in his grave.

Frank Lester emptied his glass and looked up at the large clock behind the bar. He struggled to focus and his tongue felt like it was coated with very small mushrooms. He definitely shouldn't have had that last whisky. Or probably the two before it. Or the first three for that matter. But, hey, it wasn't Christmas Eve every night. Technically it hadn't been Christmas Eve for the first four and a half hours Frank had been in the Witches, but now it was ten past midnight, so now it was Christmas Eve. Frank tried to say 'Merry Christmas', but it came out as 'Mirtle Kism' followed by a wet burp and he trailed off halfway through.

He slid off his stool and took a moment to steady himself while still holding on to the bar. Frank was a tall, willowy, pale man. His strawberry-blond hair was shaggy and needed both a trim and a wash. He wore a long, scruffy leather coat that had looked shabby when he bought it. Now it looked like a miracle of stitching that it was still together. But Frank loved that coat and wore it all year round.

Frank looked to the door. There was an alarming expanse of open space where there was nothing to hold on to. Frank really didn't want to take a tumble in front of everyone. Not that there were that many of the regulars left. Just Mick the barman, old Dr Clarence, sitting in his usual spot at the end of the bar, a face like he was chewing a particularly sour wasp, his nose in a book as always, and a handful of others Frank knew well enough to nod at in the street.

'You off then, Frank?' asked Mick, coming up to swipe Frank's empty glass. He didn't give Frank a chance to answer. He said: 'Got a Christmas joke for you, to send you on your way.' Mick was laughing before he had even started.

'There's these two cats, right? One of them's called One-Two-Three and the other one's called Un-Deux-Trois. You know, like, numbers in French.'

Frank managed the smallest of nods to show that he understood and was keeping up with the gag.

'So, anyway, they have this race, right,' Mick continued. 'Which one do you think wins?' He was straining to hold back a snigger. All Frank could manage was to shrug and shake his head. Mick hit him with the punchline: 'One-Two-Three, because Un-Deux-Trois cat sank.' And, with that, a rambunctious belly laugh bubbled up out of the depths of Mick's throat. His whole body juddered with the unbridling of his mirth. Frank frowned, playing the joke over in his head. He didn't get it. 'Un-Deux-Trois cat – Oh,

16

wait a minute!' said Mick, remembering a fairly integral part of the joke he had forgotten. 'The race, it's across a river. The cats are swimming across a river. So Un-Deux-Trois cat sank into the river. It's brilliant, innit? French cat sank. Probably drowned.'

Mick chortled and guffawed some more, oblivious to the fact that Frank hadn't so much as cracked a smile. After several moments, the power of articulate speech started to return to Frank. He nodded. 'Have a good one, Mick.'

'And you. I'll see you tomorrow,' said Mick. Frank took a deep breath and turned towards the door.

The freezing cold night air had a decent enough sobering effect and pretty soon Frank felt confident enough to start walking home. He buttoned up his coat, though it made absolutely no difference, and headed off down the street, weaving a little here and there.

At the end of the street Frank took a corner a little too wide, lost his footing and slipped over into the gutter. He gathered himself up and carried on, thinking about maybe singing. He could feel an almost overwhelming urge to start singing, which was strange because he was neither a man who liked to sing, even when alone in the shower, nor one who thought he could sing. Most people say they can't sing, but deep down inside they think they have an amazing voice. Frank opened his mouth and was about to launch into a rendition of the Oasis song 'Wonderwall' at the top of his voice when he realized he didn't know any of the words.

Frank stopped at a lamp post. He had to pee badly and this was as good a place as any. As he started, a sense of relief coursed through him.

Suddenly, he heard a *Phhrruppp!* sound and the bulb above him went out. He looked up at it and belched loudly.

*Did I do that?* he wondered. Then the neighbouring lamp, some ten metres away, went out too.

'Hmm,' said Frank, out loud.

A lamp across the road died. And then in quick succession, one by one, all the lamps in the street went dark. Within just a few seconds, the only light was coming from the moon.

Frank buttoned up his fly and was about to hurry on home when a cloud drifted across the face of the moon. He was plunged into complete darkness. He thought this was particularly spooky. Then he realized that there were absolutely no sounds around him. That made the spooky much worse and goose bumps prickled Frank's arms and the back of his neck. He was unnerved. So much so that he actually acknowledged to himself that he was unnerved.

*I'm unnerved*, he thought. It was too dark. Unnaturally dark for the city, where there was always light coming from somewhere, but Frank couldn't see any. No cars around, not even any lit windows in the surrounding houses. It was as if Frank was completely alone. The only person in the whole of Manchester.

Then he spotted a small blinking red light on the dashboard of the parked car next to him. It was a security light, blinking to inform would-be thieves that the car was alarmed. That little red light made Frank feel a bit better and a little less alone. Someone somewhere owned this car and cared enough about it to fit it with an alarm system. Or at the very least a little blinking red light. He relaxed.

Then he looked up at the lamp post again and was now sober enough to think it odd that all the lights had gone out like they had. As he was contemplating this oddity, all the bulbs in the street came back on, all at once and much brighter than before. Ten, twenty times brighter. Frank was blinded. He cried out and covered his eyes, but it was just a little too late. As he squeezed his eyes tightly shut, he could see shapes and specks drifting past his pupils, varying shades of dark and light coruscating behind his eyelids.

The lamps dimmed, returning to their usual benign luminance, but it took the best part of a minute before Frank was able to open his eyes again. Even then, he couldn't see very much. Gradually the streaks and blobs of blurred detritus swimming in his field of vision began to dissolve and his retinas ceased to sting. Frank blinked twenty-three times in quick succession and his eyes started to feel normal again.

He tilted his head to one side, frowned and squinted. There was a mound in the middle of the road that, he was pretty sure, hadn't been there a few moments before, prior to all the street lamps going supernova. The more he concentrated on it, the more he realized it was a human-shaped mound. Cautiously he moved towards it.

As he got closer he saw that the human-shaped mound was indeed a human. It was a man. Broad, with big features. A large jaw, a wide forehead. The man's hair was a dirty blond colour, and while he didn't have a full-blown beard, he clearly hadn't shaved for more than a week or maybe two. His beard was mostly the same colour as his hair but with wisps of red mixed in. He was dressed oddly: baggy cargo pants, frayed at the hems; heavy work boots, extremely worn; fingerless gloves on his hands and three dog collars around his right wrist. However, the reason Frank thought he was dressed oddly was mostly because of his jacket. It was a strange-looking jacket in itself, but it was the contrast between the jacket and the rest of his clothing that made it stand out. It was maroon with yellow horizontal stripes and matching yellow trim. On the left breast pocket was a badge. The badge read: 'My name is Anthony. How can I help?'

Frank edged closer, peering down at the prostrate man,

wondering if he was alive or not. He could see his chest rising and falling so he decided he was alive. Frank nudged him with his toe. 'Hey . . . mate . . .'

No response.

Frank's eyes flicked down to the name badge: 'Anthony . . . you awright?' He prodded him again, a bit harder this time. More a kick than a prod really. Still nothing. Frank crouched down, wobbling a bit, looking over him closely, his face just a few centimetres from Anthony's.

'You alive?'

Suddenly Anthony's eyes pinged open, taking Frank by surprise. He lost his already shaky balance and toppled over backwards with a cry.

Anthony sat up, blinking, and looked around. It was clear from his furrowed brow that he had no recollection of how he had got there.

'It was snowing,' said Anthony, articulating the first curious thing that occurred to him. Half a dozen other curious realizations also flitted through his mind at the same time, but the lack of snow seemed to be the one at the forefront.

Frank turned himself around and with some difficulty managed to sit up. Any talent he once possessed for balance had deserted him.

'Snow! Not in Manchester, mate,' he said. 'In Manchester it rains.'

Anthony turned to look at Frank. He wondered who he was but decided not to ask because there was the more pressing matter of that absent snow. Anthony looked up at the mostly cloudless sky. Frank looked up too.

The one cloud that had recently obscured the moon was on the move. It settled above them, and as Frank squinted up at it he caught sight of something small and white drifting down towards him. With marvellous precision, a snowflake floated down in a tight spiral and landed on the tip of Frank's nose. He crossed his eyes to try to look at it. He plucked it off and it dissolved between his fingers. He couldn't be sure what it had been.

However, before he could generate enough brain activity to formulate a question about what had landed on him, another snowflake entered his field of vision. Then another and another and then a million more. It was snowing. In Manchester. Where usually it only rained.

'What the . . . ?' Frank couldn't believe it. It was really snowing. Fast now. Collecting on the surfaces around him and on him.

Somewhere in the deep recesses of his mind, memories of Christmases past whirled and elided, moments from his childhood flashed past his mind's eye like images on the old slide projector his father had cherished. Frank remembered waking up on Christmas morning at his grandmother's little house in Kent and looking out of the window of his bedroom to see a blanket of snow stretching out over the fields surrounding the house. He remembered the smell of her kitchen as a turkey roasted in the oven and his grandmother arranged mince pies on a plate, sneaking sips of port and thinking no one knew. She would be drunk by lunch.

The fire crackled in the living-room hearth and his big sister sprawled on the sofa watching *The Wizard of Oz*. He remembered being scared of the flying monkeys and he remembered the sing-song tinkle of the little silver bells that hung on the Christmas tree. And then suddenly he was back in Manchester, a short time after midnight on Christmas Eve. Frank shivered, but not from the cold.

'How did you . . . ?' Frank turned to look at Anthony, but he wasn't beside him any more. He turned his head in time to see Anthony striding away, vanishing into a swirling, whirling wall of snow. Slowly Anthony faded from view, and Frank wasn't sure if he had ever really been there.

# 3

# A CIRCLE OF COBRAS

The wall was high but someone had dumped an old suitcase in the alleyway and Goose was able to position it in such a way that he could stand on it, though it smelled like a family of stray cats had been squatting in it until recently and Goose didn't want to find out what was inside. If he reached up as high as he could, there was still a gap of the best part of half a metre, but he was an athletic kid. He jumped and was able to snag his fingertips on the lip of the wall. Fortunately, no glass or other defences were embedded in the top and he was able to pull himself up, his feet scraping against the brickwork, the edges of his Converse finding a little purchase here and there where the dusty mortar had worn away over time.

His dog, now no longer a puppy, sat obediently below, watching his master scaling the wall. He was called Mutt. He was sleek, white and brown, and had big, expressive eyes that missed nothing. He glanced quickly left and right as if he was keeping lookout.

Goose peered over the top into the dark garden beyond. The light of the moon reflected off the snow that was lying all around and still falling. The garden was small, like all the backyards in this part of Manchester, but unlike most of them this one was lovingly maintained, with narrow pathways that traversed bushes and rockeries from which unusual statues looked out. The statues were of Hindu gods but Goose didn't know that. There were areas of lawn and gravel separated by small evergreen border hedges. He could see strings of dormant fairy lights were strung around the whole garden.

His breath clouded as he exhaled, sitting on top of the wall. He looked different. Older than the year that had passed since the crash. His wild, all-over-the-place hair was long gone. In its place was a military-style buzz cut. He had lost weight from his face and he looked sullen. He still had huge green eyes, but there was no joy behind them any more. He had nothing to be joyful about. A near-permanent frown pushed his thick eyebrows closer together.

He could see into the neighbouring yards on both sides. A large, circular trampoline dominated the one on his left. The safety net around the trampoline was tatty and torn. The ground was littered with junk. The yard on the right was decked and there was a two-storey playhouse in one corner. Clearly children lived in both of these houses. Goose looked up at the house to his right: three windows on the first floor. He imagined one of the children waking from a bad dream and crying out, the father jumping out of bed and hurrying across the hallway, kneeling down and stroking his son's brow, pushing the hair out of his eyes and telling him to go back to sleep because everything was all right.

Goose felt weight in the pit of his stomach, as if a jagged ball of stone was expanding within him, pulling him down. He knew, for the rest of his life, there would never be anyone to comfort him like that. He tried to convince himself that he didn't need it, but the lie didn't fool him for a second. All he could do was choose not to dwell on it. Mutt yapped once, breaking Goose's train of thought and pulling him out of his brooding. The stone ball contracted once again, but it would be back sooner or later.

'Sorry, Mutt,' whispered Goose.

He looked down and could see a bench in the garden beneath him. He pushed himself off the wall and landed in an empty flower bed. The snow crunched under his feet. Crouching down, Goose observed the house. There was no movement or sign of life. He moved swiftly across the yard to a pair of French windows and retrieved a small torch from his jacket pocket. He switched it on and shone it through the glass.

He was looking into a living room. The beam from the torch landed on a chunky, antiquated television set and a stereo. Neither was worth very much, if anything, and Goose rarely stole bulky items like that. Too heavy to carry, too hard to conceal if stopped by the coppers.

Goose was close to deciding to call it a night when the beam from his torch hit something that glinted. He stopped and moved back slowly. As the beam crossed the arm of an old worn leather chair, there was another glint of light. Goose squinted and saw a gold bangle sitting there.

Goose heard Mutt bark softly once again from the other side of the wall. He pulled an old Swiss Army knife that had once belonged to his dad out of his pocket and forced the blade into a gap by the lock. One quick, much-practised flick of his wrist and the door opened. It always shocked Goose just how easy it was to break into most houses. He opened the door and stepped inside.

The house smelled a little musty. Someone elderly lived here. For a split second Goose thought about his nan at home alone right now. He quickly pushed those thoughts out of his head and concentrated on the job at hand.

He crossed to the armchair and directed the beam of his torch on to the bangle. He picked it up and examined it in the light. It was beautiful. It was gold. Old gold. Goose could tell the difference. There was weight to it. The bangle was in the shape of two cobras in a circle, each biting the other's tail. The detail was exquisite. Every scale on the snakes' skin had been individually outlined and the torchlight surged through the minute fissures like flowing lava.

He heard floorboards creaking upstairs. He froze and listened. He couldn't hear anyone moving. Maybe it was just someone turning over in bed.

Goose looked around. There was nothing else of value so he left, closing the door behind him.

He made his way back across the small garden. The falling snow had already filled in his footprints from earlier and he knew that soon there would be no trace of him. He climbed up on to the back of the bench and jumped towards the high back wall, got his hands on the top and pulled himself up and over.

He dropped down into the alleyway, where Mutt was waiting for him. The dog yapped. Just then they heard the sound of a car approaching and they froze. Goose stared at the mouth of the alleyway. He felt the drumming of his heart: partly from the exertion of climbing the wall and partly from the fear of being caught. The car was drawing ever closer. It was moving slowly. Goose imagined a police car, moving slowly because its occupants were looking for someone. Maybe he had been spotted sitting on top of the wall earlier. Goose looked behind him to the other end of the alleyway. It was a long way and the alleyway was wide enough for a car to drive down. If the police chased him, he'd have no chance of escaping. The car was close now. Goose held his breath. A taxi drove past. Its tyres were slipping and sliding on the snowy tarmac, which was why it was moving slowly. Goose breathed a sigh of relief as it disappeared from view.

'Come on, Mutt,' said Goose, rising to his feet. 'It's cold. Let's go home.' He moved to the mouth of the alleyway and leaned out. He saw the tail lights of the taxi disappearing in the distance and nothing else. Goose trudged off into the night with Mutt trotting beside him.

# 4

# A TURKEY IN THE WASHING MACHINE

Daylight poured in through the thin floral-print curtains and Goose woke up, feeling like he had only just got to bed, which wasn't so far from the truth. He was still wearing his clothes and one of his Converse trainers. Mutt was curled up in a tight little ball at the foot of the bed.

Goose rolled over and yelped as he lay on something hard. He reached underneath the small of his back and pulled out the bangle. He held it up and examined it once again. The workmanship was excellent. This wasn't factory made. There was lettering around the inside, but Goose didn't recognize the language. There were straight, horizontal lines at the top of most of the words, then, beneath curves and squiggles, lots of what looked like the number three. A beam of light snuck in through a gap in the curtains and struck the head of one of the cobras, causing its eyes to flare as if they were bejewelled, but they were not. For a few moments Goose was mesmerized by the bangle, but then he tossed it on to his jacket, which was sitting on a nearby chair, and sat up, stretched and yawned.

He lived in his nan's house now. For a few days after the accident Nan had stayed with Goose in his house, but it was rented and she had said she couldn't afford to keep paying for it. She only had her pension. So, early in the New Year, Goose had gathered all his possessions into three boxes and two black bin bags and now this was where he lived. He had put the boxes, which were mostly full of toys, straight into the cupboard in the corner of his room. He had not opened them once in the last year. His bedroom was about half the size of his old room. It was just as untidy, but looked cold and less lived in. The walls were bare. No posters any more. There were still plenty of books lying around. Clothes, magazines, dirty plates and bowls littered the floor.

Goose knelt up on the bed and pulled back the curtain. It had stopped snowing now, but a thick, brilliant blanket covered everything in sight. Nan's little house was just one of many in a sprawling estate built in the sixties. The

31

houses were beige, the roads were grey and concrete covered everything. There was no greenery, even in the height of summer, no trees to blossom in spring or leaves to redden in the autumn. Goose couldn't imagine a more drab and uninspiring vista anywhere in the world. He had seen a documentary on TV about Chernobyl, and he remembered thinking it looked more inviting than where he lived. However, today was different. The depressing view that usually greeted him had been replaced with a magical landscape straight out of Narnia. Most of the neighbourhood kids were already out there having more fun than they had ever had: making snowmen and engaging in frenzied snowball fights. Goose watched them dispassionately. He neither envied them nor wanted to join them nor felt irritated by them. He felt nothing at all.

After the crash, Goose had experienced more grief than he could have imagined possible. He had sobbed for days. His eyes stung from crying and his throat felt bone dry. When he couldn't cry any more, his grief turned to anger. He wanted to scream at the top of his lungs. He wanted to destroy anything and everything. One time in a burst of rage he had kicked Mutt. The little dog had yelped and scurried away, looking shocked, scared and betrayed. Goose was immediately horrified by what he had done. More than that, he was horrified by the fact that he had done it knowingly. It wasn't a spur-of-the-moment reaction. He had thought about it. He had had time to stop himself, but he had done it anyway. He had wanted to hurt someone or something. And he had.

He'd picked up Mutt gently and held him, stroking him lovingly and apologizing over and over again. Mutt wasn't the sort of dog to hold a grudge. He had licked Goose's face and nipped his ear playfully. That was the first time Goose had laughed since his parents died. There hadn't been a second time yet. As a reaction to hurting Mutt, Goose put away his anger. He locked it up, deep inside himself, and threw away the key. Unfortunately every other emotion had to go with it. That's just how it worked with Goose: lose one, lose them all.

He let the curtain fall back into place and climbed off the bed. He found his other trainer and put it on.

Mutt was awake, watching his master. He yawned and waited to see what Goose would do.

'Come on, Mutt,' said Goose as he grabbed his jacket and left the room. Mutt jumped up and followed.

Goose plodded down the narrow staircase; Mutt trotted after. Whatever youthful exuberance Goose once possessed was all but gone. There was a time when he would dash everywhere, always looking to escape, but he didn't rush anywhere any more. There was nowhere he wanted to be in any particular sort of hurry.

At school, when he went, he rarely spoke to anyone and kept to himself at break times. At first, both teachers and pupils were sympathetic to his situation. The headmaster had made a moving speech during assembly, urging everyone to give Goose the space he so clearly craved. Then, over time, that just became the way everyone interacted with him. Teachers stopped calling on him to answer questions in class. Not that he ever put his hand up. The other kids didn't even think about approaching him to see if he wanted to play. Goose knew all the quiet, out-of-the-way places in his school. The places he could go and not be disturbed.

Over the last year only one significant event had occurred at school that involved Goose. It was when a new kid started. His name was Darren and he had arrived in Manchester from somewhere south. He was big for his age and had decided his role at school was to be respected through fear. He set out to be a bully and, out of all the people he could have chosen, he picked on Goose to assert his dominance.

He came up behind Goose as he was walking across the playground one lunchtime. Goose was on his way to a small roof behind the gym that practically no one knew about or even thought about if they saw it. Darren shoved Goose viciously. So hard in fact that Goose pitched forward. Goose's hands were in his pockets and he ripped his jacket in a desperate attempt to get at least one hand free to control his fall. It could have been a lot worse, but he still scraped up one side of his chin and the palm of the hand that he put out to stop himself.

Goose fought back the tears as Darren loomed over him. The new boy sneered down at him.

'They say you lost your mum and dad. Bit bloody careless of ya, weren' it?' Darren had spent most of the morning thinking up what he was going to say. He grinned at all the kids nearby who had stopped to watch. Had he been paying more attention to Goose he would have noticed him get up and launch a tightly clenched fist straight at his face. It connected, shattering Darren's nose and causing him to bite down through his own tongue. Blood gushed out of his nostrils and from his mouth. Darren hated the sight of his own blood and started shrieking and flapping his arms. Unfortunately for Darren that was the image that stayed with all the onlookers, and from then on his nickname was Scream Queen. Screamer or Queenie for short.

Goose put up no defence when questioned by the headmaster, and it was only several of the other students' saying that Darren had incited the whole thing that meant Goose wasn't permanently excluded.

However, following that episode Goose was labelled a 'troublemaker' in the minds of the teaching staff and that's how they treated him.

Goose reached the bottom of the stairs, turned left and made his way along the dark hallway to the small kitchen at the end. As he entered he saw his nan hunched over the washing machine. She was wrestling with a large turkey, trying to force it in through the door of the machine. Nan had Alzheimer's. It'd been getting worse over the last few years, and when Goose's mum and dad were alive his mum was becoming increasingly worried. However, before the accident Nan could still function normally most of the time. Her condition generally manifested itself in an overwhelming desire to organize and tidy. Sometimes her episodes were funny and even useful, like the time she'd arranged everything in the old kitchen by colour and size. Other times they weren't so funny and not at all useful, like when she hung all Dad's tropical fish on the clothes line to dry. Though it was a little funny that she had also hung out frozen fish fingers at the same time.

Since the accident, Nan's condition was worsening by the day and Goose didn't know what to do. It was amazing that no one had noticed and come calling. Goose assumed they had *'slipped through the cracks of the system'*. That's the sort of thing he heard on the news all the time. Though usually it was in connection with some horrible tragedy. Goose was pleased that the system was failing them. He knew Nan needed help, but what would happen to him if she left? He would be put into care, and he was pretty sure he wouldn't be allowed to keep Mutt. He knew this couldn't go on much longer. He would work out what to do. Soon. But not today.

'What're you doing, Nan?' Goose asked.

Nan gave a little startled yelp and turned to look at him. 'Oh, Goose, you gave me a fright. Didn't hear you come in. Morning, you two, sleep well?'

'What are you doing, Nan?' Goose repeated.

'What do you mean, love?' said Nan, a sweet-little-old-lady smile on her sweet-little-old-lady lips. Nan was small and white-haired, comfortably plump and rosy-cheeked. She looked like the perfect fairytale grandmother. Except Goose couldn't remember any fairytales where the grandmother forced turkeys into washing machines.

'What're you doing with that turkey, Nan?' said Goose.

Nan looked down at the bird in her hand and frowned. *What a silly question*, she thought.

'Well, it's not going to cook itself, is it, darling?'

'That's the washing machine, Nan,' said Goose.

He saw Nan's features darken as she glanced at the washing machine, then at the turkey, then at the oven on the other side of the kitchen. He could see the moment writ large on Nan's face when she realized her mistake. She looked horribly sad.

'Oh. Silly old fool,' said Nan in a tiny, pathetic voice.

Goose crossed and took the turkey from her. He laid it on the kitchen table and led Nan to a chair.

'Don't worry, Nan, it's only Christmas Eve,' he said, forcing a warm and cheery tone into his voice.

'Is it?' asked Nan.

Goose thought she was about to start crying and he desperately wanted to get out before that happened. 'Easy mistake to make. I'll help you. We'll do it together. Tomorrow. Yeah?'

Nan nodded and forced a weak smile.

'I'll see you later, Nan. Come on, Mutt.' Goose edged to the door, itching to leave, but then he stopped and looked back. His nan was staring down at the chequered pattern of the Formica on the kitchen tabletop and wringing an old tea towel between her fingers. Goose wished he knew the right thing to say: the thing that would help Nan and make her all better again. There was nothing, so he bit the inside of his cheek and left.

Nan watched Goose and Mutt leaving. Her brain felt foggy, though she hadn't noticed until Goose had pointed out her mistake with the turkey. She hated that this was happening to her, but she couldn't seem to make it stop. Most of all she felt that she was failing Goose. She knew he was beyond miserable, though he always kept a breezy, cheery tone to his voice when he spoke to her. She loved him all the more

38

for that. She knew he was sneaking out at night. Part of her knew what he was getting up to, but right now she couldn't really remember. Her mind was like someone tuning a radio. Every now and again a clear signal would emerge from the static.

It was a year ago to the very day that her son and daughter-in-law had died. She had meant to say something to Goose. Maybe he had wanted to mark the day somehow. They could visit the cemetery. A fleeting moment of clarity told her that he wouldn't want that. He hadn't visited their graves once that she knew of. Of course that didn't mean anything. He did lots of things that she didn't know about, but she had tried on occasion to talk to him about his parents and he would always find some way to end the conversation as quickly as possible. She knew she should force the issue, but her mind just wasn't flexible enough any more to even try. She cursed her failing faculties. She was useless.

Her mind wandered, drifting back to the village in Norfolk to which she had been evacuated during the war. She remembered the church that looked over the village green and the bicycle she had been given by the couple she had stayed with. They were called Muriel and Ainsley Fenchurch. He was the first person she had ever met with a beard, and she had a large mole growing on her chin and smelled of rose water. They had a dog called Barney, a red setter. She remembered the apple tree at the bottom of their garden. She could even picture the red hue of the apples and still taste their tartness as she sank her teeth into them. She could remember the chickens clucking on the Galbraith farm, which was down the road from the Fenchurches' house, left, right and then left again. She would cycle to it at least twice a week to pick up eggs. She could remember the feel of the cloth of the blue and green dress Mrs Fenchurch had made for her rubbing against her thighs as she pedalled. She could remember all that so vividly and yet she couldn't manage to concentrate for five blasted minutes to talk to her grandson and make sure he was okay. She thumped her fist on the table and tears pooled in her eyes.

# 5

# SHOWDOWN AT THE SWINGS

For the majority of the year, Beech Road Park was a small oasis of greenery in the Chorlton area of Manchester. It was surrounded on all sides by houses and was a favourite place for the neighbourhood kids to congregate. They had been there all morning and thick snow had been sculpted into an army of snowmen of varying sizes. Most of the kids had gone now – off home for a snack or an early lunch – but they'd be back.

Darryl Craig and Carl Mills, Millsy to his friends, were sixteen and seventeen respectively. Darryl was tall and skinny, while Millsy was taller and flabby. They had been friends since they were three years old and had moved

41

in opposite one another on the Joshua Tree Estate. They had no idea why it was called that. Darryl had looked up the Joshua Tree once, and beyond it being the name of an album by U2 and a plant that grew in the Mojave Desert in America, he had no clue why someone had chosen to name their estate after it.

They walked through the park karate-kicking the snowmen. In their heads they were ninja assassins fighting the evil forces of the Supreme Overlord, battling his warriors, making their way to him. There was one snowman right in the centre of the park that was larger than all the rest. This was the Supreme Overlord. Millsy and Darryl reached him, having defeated his minions, and now had to face their greatest foe. Unfortunately their joint imaginations didn't really extend beyond giving the snowman a right good kicking, and pretty soon the Supreme Overlord was just a pile of snow in the midst of other piles of snow, and Millsy and Darryl were cold and bored.

They sat on a concrete plinth that used to sport a memorial to Queen Victoria, but it had been defaced and vandalized so often that the council removed it. They were trying to ignore the cold. This was easier for Millsy, who had a heavy army-surplus trench coat. Darryl was wearing a thin Adidas hoodie, because that was all he had.

They saw a figure walking across their battlefield,

turning in circles, looking lost. It was Anthony. Millsy and Darryl watched him approaching.

'What's this numpty about?' said Darryl, sticking out his chin in Anthony's direction and making sure to keep his hands in his pockets.

'Nice jacket,' replied Millsy with a smile out of one side of his mouth. 'Looks like a right perv.'

Anthony saw the two youths ahead of him. He had seen them from the moment he entered the park. He was careful to keep them in sight but not project a defensive air. He knew it didn't pay to provoke people looking for trouble, and the world was full of them. At the same time maybe he was being unfair. Just because they looked like a pair of ASBO-collecting yobs, it didn't mean they were. He planned to walk past, but then one of them called out to him.

'You all right there, pal?' called Darryl. 'You look a little lost.'

Anthony didn't make eye contact, but he was subtle about it. He shook his head. 'It's not right. Something's not right.'

'I can tell you something that's not right,' said Millsy with a smile directed at Darryl, who returned it.

'This is Manchester,' said Anthony.

'Yeah,' agreed Millsy.

'I wasn't here, but now I am.' Anthony was talking

as much to himself as to Millsy and Darryl. The two boys exchanged a look.

'Don't worry about it, pal,' said Darryl. 'It's Christmas. It's okay to get a little merry at Christmas.'

Anthony frowned as he thought about it. He held his hand to his mouth and breathed into his palm. His breath wasn't great, smelled a bit medicinal and there was something else. Peanuts. Dry-roasted. But no odour of alcohol.

'No, I haven't been drinking,' said Anthony. 'But I have been eating dry-roasted peanuts, which are an ingredient in dynamite.' Why did he say that? Where had it come from? It just came out. He thought about it. Couldn't remember how he knew it, but he was pretty sure it was true.

Millsy and Darryl looked at one another, both thinking the same thing: *Is this guy a nutter or can we have some fun with him?*

'That's interesting, isn't it, Millsy?' said Darryl.

'Millsy,' said Anthony. He could feel his brain starting to function independently of the rest of him. It was if an exterior force was controlling him. He knew he was about to say something, but he wasn't sure what. 'Mills. Windmills. Always turn anticlockwise.' The two boys were staring at him. He understood. He would have been staring too if he was where they were. 'Except in Ireland.' He felt like he was finished for now.

44

'Why's that?' asked Millsy.

Anthony shrugged. 'No idea.'

'Live round here, do you?' Darryl asked.

'No.' Anthony blinked. 'I don't think I do.'

'You saying you don't know where you live?' asked Millsy. But before Anthony could answer a sly thought sprang into his head and he added, 'Check your wallet.' Darryl and Millsy glanced at each other. In that instant the plan was set: *drunk bloke gets out his wallet, we grab it and scarper.*

'Wallet!' exclaimed Anthony. What a brilliant idea. Why hadn't he thought of it? Everything in his head was very mixed up. He started patting his pockets. He had many. Eight in his baggy cargo pants alone. He looked glum and shook his head. 'No wallet.'

Darryl and Millsy were disappointed. 'Mobile?' asked Darryl. It was better than nothing.

Anthony checked his pockets again, this time pulling out the contents. It was mostly worthless junk.

'Biro, blue. Box of matches. Another box of matches. A sock.' Anthony paused to give the sock a quick sniff. It reeked so he shoved it back in his pocket, but he could still smell it. The smell was lodged in his nose. He knew it would creep slowly into the back of his throat and then he'd be able to taste it too. Yeah, there it was. He stuck out his tongue, breathing out to try to expel the bitter sting of old sock. He continued to itemize his possessions. 'Another box of matches. God! I must smoke a lot. A poker chip. Hmm, interesting.' Anthony couldn't remember being in a casino, though he ran through the rules of blackjack in his head and was surprised to discover that he did know how to play. He carried on searching. He pulled out a Pez dispenser in the shape of Scooby-Doo. 'Ooh! Pez.' He took one, popped it in his mouth to combat the taste of the sock and held it out to Millsy and Darryl. 'Pez?' he offered.

They shook their heads, both becoming a little impatient. This guy was clearly just an old tramp and they wouldn't get anything worthwhile from him.

'Ooh, hello. What's this?' said Anthony, ferreting deep down into a pocket somewhere around his knee. He drew out his hand and opened it to reveal a gold cigarette lighter. Millsy and Darryl perked up: at last something worthwhile. They knew a bloke in the open market who would buy anything gold. No questions asked. Probably wouldn't give them what it was worth, but it'd be better than nothing.

'That real gold?' asked Millsy.

'I think so,' replied Anthony.

All three of them looked down at the lighter sitting in the palm of Anthony's hand for a few moments and then suddenly Darryl's hand shot out, like a rattlesnake in one of those BBC documentaries launching itself at an unsuspecting rodent. Darryl's hand was a blur of movement, but by the time it reached Anthony's palm the lighter wasn't there any more. It had vanished before their very eyes.

Anthony opened his other hand to reveal the cigarette lighter. He looked like a bemused magician.

'How'd I do that?' he asked aloud.

'Give us it 'ere!' snapped Darryl, anger rising in him as he suspected Anthony was making fun of him. He threw himself at Anthony's other hand, grabbed his wrist and prised open his fingers. The lighter had vanished once more.

Anthony shook his head. 'I really don't know how I'm doing that,' he said.

Millsy jumped into the fray to help his friend. What happened next was confusing for all involved. Anthony twisted his body and whirled around Millsy, who stumbled forward. He ended up in the arms of his friend. They looked as if they were about to kiss. The two boys jerked back from one another only to discover that Anthony had somehow managed to loop their watchstraps together.

'Hey!' cried Darryl.

'How'd you do that?' Millsy asked Anthony.

Anthony shrugged. 'Honestly, no idea.'

'Don't pull, you idiot. You'll break it!' Darryl snapped at his friend. They took a moment to unhook themselves.

Anthony started to wander away, not remotely concerned by these two young thugs, even though they were clearly riled up now. Darryl and Millsy swaggered after him.

'You looking for a slap, pal?' asked Darryl through gritted teeth.

'No,' replied Anthony. 'I remember the sea.'

This threw Millsy and Darryl a little. What did the sea have to do with anything?

'Get him!' barked Darryl, and he and Millsy pounced on Anthony. Anthony shifted his weight and, almost like a dancer, spun out of their path. In one swift movement, he grabbed the hem at the back of Millsy's thick woollen coat and pulled it up and over the boy's head. The coat twisted inside out and stretched across Millsy's chest, incapacitating him as if he was entwined in a strange sort of straitjacket.

Darryl threw a punch, but Anthony caught his fist easily and twisted his arm, spinning Darryl around. The teenager cried out in pain.

'You're a nutter!' he shouted.

'Very possibly,' said Anthony calmly. He let go of Darryl's wrist and the boy started running. Millsy watched his friend deserting him.

'Darryl!' he cried, but Darryl didn't stop or look back. Millsy struggled to escape from his own coat and the moment he was free he ran too, leaving the coat lying in the snow behind him. Anthony picked it up.

'Hey!' he called. 'You left your coat.' But Darryl was

long gone and he saw Millsy vanish through some bushes. Anthony waited for a few moments, but it didn't look like the boys were coming back. He shrugged and threw the coat on over his maroon and yellow jacket. *Waste not, want not*, he thought. It fitted perfectly, and he walked away.

# 6
# FRANK THE FENCE

Frank lay entwined in his duvet, wearing only a mangy pair of Y-fronts and his prized David Bowie *Aladdin Sane* T-shirt. His head was tilted backwards, his mouth hung open and a deep, sonorous roar drifted up from the depths of his throat. Somewhere he could hear banging: *bang bang bangbangbang bangbangbangbang bang bang!* It replayed over and over again. *Bang bang bangbangbang bangbangbangbang bang bang!*

'Sharrup!' Frank managed to croak.

*Bang bang bangbangbang bangbangbangbang bang bang!*

This time it got through to the meat of Frank's brain and he lifted his head off the pillow and managed to open one eye almost all the way.

Frank flung open the bedroom door and stomped out, trying to wrap a brown towelling dressing gown around himself as he headed along the narrow hallway to his front door.

*Bang bang bangbangbang bangbangbangbang bang bang!*

'All right! All right! Knock it off, will ya? I'm coming,' Frank shouted. The banging stopped. 'Who is it?' he asked.

He heard Goose's voice on the other side of the door. 'Hurry up, will ya, Frank? It's bloody freezin' out 'ere.' Frank gave his face a rub in some half-arsed attempt to get the blood flowing and unlocked the door. Goose and Mutt were standing on his doorstep.

'It snowed,' said Goose, jabbing a finger over his shoulder at the frozen view from the walkway outside Frank's eighth-floor council flat.

'Yeah, I know,' said Frank, as the events of the previous night started to come back to him. He remembered the strange man in the maroon-and-yellow jacket lying in the road. He wondered for a moment if that had been a dream. He didn't think so but wasn't a hundred per cent.

Goose stepped inside and Mutt started to follow. Frank quickly put his bare foot in the path of the dog, barring his entry.

'I've told you before, Goose: I don't wan' him in 'ere.'

'Ah, come on, Frank. Look, he's shivering.' They both

looked down at Mutt, who wasn't shivering in the slightest, but, almost as if he could understand what Goose was saying, he started quaking and looking pathetic. He even let out a sad little whine.

'Don't push it, Goose. I've got the worst bloody hangover,' growled Frank.

'Yeah, you do look grey,' said Goose, staring at Frank's bloodshot eyes and lifeless complexion. He turned to Mutt. 'Stay here, Mutt. I won't be long.' Mutt lay down on the doormat and curled up into a little ball to wait as Goose headed inside and Frank closed the door.

Goose followed Frank into the darkened living room. Frank drew back the curtains and immediately wished he hadn't. The sunlight reflected off the snow outside, blinding him. His hangover throbbed angrily behind his eyes. Frank redrew one side of the curtains and slumped down on his sofa.

Beer cans, bottles, pizza boxes and takeaway cartons were everywhere. Packing cases were stacked along one wall. Frank had been living here for the best part of a year, but he still hadn't really unpacked. He wasn't sure he'd ever get around to it, but that was mostly because, even after all this time, he still hadn't come to terms with being here and not there. There being home with his wife, Alice, and their daughter, Jemma.

He saw Goose looking at some photo albums open

52

on the coffee table. Inside were pictures of Frank and his estranged family. Goose didn't need to say anything. He knew that Frank had been wallowing in his own misery the night before. Same as he did every night. Frank reddened with embarrassment, but then he noticed that Goose was only looking at one of the photos. It showed Frank in mid-flight alongside his best friend as the two of them bombed into a swimming pool on holiday in Corfu when they were in their early twenties. Frank's best friend had been Paul, Goose's dad. He and Frank had known one another since their school days. Goose was Frank's godson. A thought flitted through Frank's mind: would Paul approve of what he and Goose were doing? Frank told himself that he was doing it for the right reasons. Goose would be doing this with or without him. This way Frank could keep an eye on him and make sure he didn't get hurt. Frank quickly shut the albums and moved them aside. Goose looked away and noticed an ugly brown stain on the carpet. He didn't want to know what had made that.

'What've you got then?' Frank asked.

Goose started emptying his pockets: various pieces of jewellery, iPods, a couple of mobile phones, a glass eyeball and the cobra bangle. Goose thought for a moment and then quickly pocketed the eyeball again.

Frank leaned forward and rooted through the pile of swag with a finger, looking at it all somewhat dismissively.

Then, almost against his will, his hand was drawn towards the bangle. He held it up to the light and for a moment seemed mesmerized by its beauty.

'Nice, eh?' said Goose, looking for approval.

Realizing he was tipping his hand, Frank chastised himself silently. He had just broken the first rule in the fence's handbook. He tossed the bangle back on the pile and shrugged indifferently.

''S'all right. Nothing special. You can pick that sort of thing up all over the shop.'

Goose rankled. 'Yeah? Not that I've seen.'

Frank sifted through the loot, separating everything into two piles. The last item he allocated was the bangle and he made a pantomime of choosing where it should go. This pile? That pile? This pile? That pile? Finally he tossed it unceremoniously on to the right-hand pile.

'This stuff . . .' said Frank, pointing to the pile on the right, 'it's not bad. Not great, but not bad. This stuff . . .' the left-hand pile, 'cack!'

'What're you talkin' about?' said Goose indignantly. 'What about them phones? And that iPod; nothin' wrong wi' that!'

Frank sighed, forcing the paternal patience of his voice, making sure that Goose didn't miss his point.

'I've told you before, Goose, no one wants straight mobiles these days. I couldn't give 'em away . . . 'less it was as a free gift with an iPhone!' Goose looked deflated. Frank smiled sympathetically. 'I'll tell ya what, seeing as it's Christmas, I'll give you fifty for the lot.'

Goose frowned. 'Fifty! You havin' a laugh?'

'It's a fair price,' said Frank.

Goose's brow furrowed some more and he sat looking at Frank, breathing heavily, his anger rising. 'No, it's not!' Seething, he started to gather everything together, jamming it all back into his pockets. 'Don't do me no favours, yeah, Frank. You don't wan' it, I'll just go see what Kermit'll give us for it.'

Suddenly Frank became deadly serious and grabbed Goose's wrist. He held him a little too hard. 'I've told you before about that Kermit. Stay away from him. He's a right headcase.'

'You can't tell me what to do, Frank; you're not me dad!'

Frank's jaw tensed. He tightened his grip on Goose's arm and his mind raced as he debated how to deal with this. It was more than he could handle: Christmas Eve morning, and with a marching band playing vuvuzelas passing through his head. He let go of Goose's arm and nodded.

'Fair enough, Goose. I'll give you seventy.'

'Hundred,' said Goose without missing a beat.

'Okay, eighty. Final offer.'

'Hundred,' said Goose again. He was now angry

enough to actually take this stuff to Kermit. He wasn't going to back down. Fortunately, he didn't have to.

Frank shook his head. "Aven't quite got hagglin' yet, have ya? All right, hundred it is. But you promise me you won't have nothin' to do with that Kermit and his lot. Promise me, Goose.'

Goose couldn't remember Frank being so passionate about anything before, but he still wasn't quite ready to back down. He stalled for time by running the back of his hand under his nose. The move from the cold air outside to the warmer air had made his nose run.

'You promise me on your dad's memory.' Frank stared Goose in the eye. He'd never used that before, and evoking his dad's name made the fight bleed out of Goose. Goose nodded.

'Yeah, okay, Frank. I promise.'


Frank followed Goose along the hallway towards the front door. Goose was counting through the money Frank had just given him.

'God's sake, Goose, it's all there,' said Frank, clearly put out.

'You're the one always said count it.'

'I didn't mean from me though, did I?'

Goose stopped counting and shoved the wad of tenners into a pocket. They reached the front door and Goose went to pull back the lock but he stopped. He turned back to Frank, but couldn't quite look at him. 'What you doin' tomorrow?' he asked.

Frank looked uncomfortable. He shuffled his feet. 'I'm not sure yet. I might have to see a man about some stuff.'

Goose nodded, awkwardly. 'If you want, you could come over to our place. Can't guarantee turkey'll be cooked, but it'll probably be clean.' Goose smiled to himself, but Frank didn't get it.

Frank nodded. 'Yeah, maybe. I'll see.'

Goose unlocked the door. He was about to step outside when Frank said: 'But thanks.' And Goose knew he meant it. Goose left, closing the door behind him.

The shock of the cold made Goose's skin feel as if it was being stretched tight across his face. He wrapped his arms around himself and looked down, expecting to see Mutt. He wasn't there. Goose looked along the straight walkway. First one way and then the other.

'Mutt!' he called. 'Where are you, you dumb dog?' He whistled and waited. Mutt didn't come running. That was odd. Mutt always came running. 'Come on, Mutt!' He waited some more, and as he did panic was just starting to rise inside him. Mutt never wandered away. Not very far at least. The logical part of Goose's brain was telling him that there was a very simple explanation for where Mutt had got to, but that part of his brain was being shouted down by the other part. The part that was all passion and no logic. He and Mutt had not been apart for a single full day in the year since he'd got him. Goose always knew where he was. Even when Goose went to school he would run home and Mutt would be waiting for him. Goose couldn't count on his nan. Her Alzheimer's made her unpredictable. Mutt wasn't unpredictable. He was the only constant left in Goose's life. His reaction wasn't logical, but it was inevitable. 'MUTT!' he called, louder this time.

Goose started towards the stairs, thinking maybe Mutt had ducked in there to get out of the wind and he couldn't hear him calling. But when he reached the steps there was no sign of him.

Goose stepped back to the walkway and looked over. He had a bird's eye view, but there was no sign of Mutt anywhere.

'MUTT!'

He looked straight down and caught sight of footprints in the snow, or at least what he thought were footprints, or paw prints rather. He turned and ran. He hit the stairs and bounded down the eight flights as quickly as he could, jumping the last three or four steps each time.

Soon he reached the ground floor and raced out into the snow. The paw prints he had seen from up above were a mishmash of a hundred sets of footprints, paw prints and bike tracks.

Goose started running, but he had no idea in which direction to go. He headed off the estate into the road. As he came out he could see for a good half-mile east and west. No sign of Mutt.

Goose stood in the middle of the road, turning in a circle.

'Mutt!' he cried. 'Where are ya? Come 'ere, boy! Come 'ere, Mutt! *Please!*'

Still nothing. Choosing a direction at random, he started running again.

# 7

# LEONARDO DA VINCI INVENTED SCISSORS

Lal Premji had taken her cobra bangle off, but where? She remembered her wrist had been aching the night before. Sometimes her bangle seemed heavy. She had taken it off. Yes, she distinctly remembered taking it off. It was a tight squeeze to remove it. Didn't used to be. Not in her youth, when Meher had given it to her. She was a slim, lithe young thing back then. Over the years she had plumped up a little; she blamed her love of custard creams.

She was seventy-six years old. A tall woman, though a little stooped with age. She had short hair, silver peppered with some black, and wore a pair of browline glasses.

She had come to this country from the Gujerati region of north-western India in her twenties. She had been here, in the north of England, for fifty-four years and, after living through fifty-four freezing, wet winters and summers not much better, she still loved the cold. Growing up in India she had always been too hot. Back there, she felt sluggish and tired. Here it was like a million freezing needles pricking her. She felt alert.

Today, though, she wasn't enjoying the cold. It rarely snowed in Manchester, and the few times she had experienced snow she had loved it. Felt like a kid. Today, however, was different. Today she was padding through the white streets in her slippered feet, wearing a thick green cardigan she had knitted for her husband some fifteen years ago, searching the pavements and gutters, retracing her steps from the day before. What had she done? She had gone to the post office in the morning and sent a birthday card to her niece, Asha, who lived in Toronto with a very boring man called Tim. After the post office she had stopped off at the library to change her books. If she had taken it off while she was out, then she would have put it into her bag. But she had gone through her bag. Tipped it out on the kitchen table. It definitely wasn't there. That thought made her heart ache. If it had fallen out of her bag, would she have noticed? And why did it have to snow last night of all nights? It made her search so much harder. Her bangle

61

could be next to her but covered in a thick layer of snow so she would never know.

She turned the corner of Sutherland Road and saw the bus stop ahead. She had walked from the library to the bus stop. She retraced her steps, scanning the ground as she went.

There was a young woman at the bus stop with a toddler in a buggy, which was loaded down with shopping. 'You all right, love?' she asked. Lal looked up at her with teary eyes. 'Is something the matter?'

'I've lost a bangle. It's gold. In the shape of two snakes. It's very precious to me. I can't think where I could have lost it. I've been retracing my steps from yesterday.' After fifty-four years there was only the merest hint of her native Gujerati accent left in her voice. Lal sounded Mancunian now.

The young woman looked around her. She saw a drain and crossed to it, peering down into the darkness. She frowned. 'What's that?' she asked.

Lal went over and looked down too. Both women saw something glinting, something metallic, in the shadows of the drain, but couldn't make out what it was. Lal's heart leaped. Could it be her bangle? She dropped to her knees, taking the young woman by surprise.

'Maybe I should do that,' she said.

Lal smiled. 'You're very sweet, love, but you don't

want to get all mucky.' She threaded her fingers through the grating and stretched her hand down as far as it would go, but the glinting object was agonizingly just out of her reach. She gave up. 'Can't reach it!'

The young woman was a good bit shorter than Lal, so there was no way she would be able to reach it if Lal couldn't. She looked around and saw a man in a heavy trench coat on the other side of the road. He was staring up at a building site opposite.

''Scuse me! 'Allo!' she called.

Anthony turned to look. Was that young woman calling to him? He looked around and didn't see anyone else so he crossed the street. As he drew closer, the old Indian lady got to her feet with the young woman's assistance.

'Where are the flats?' asked Anthony, pointing at the building site.

'What?' said the young woman. 'No, they haven't built them yet.'

'But I remember them,' said Anthony, looking bewildered.

'There used to be an old factory there. They knocked it down . . . to build flats.'

Anthony looked across the street to the building site. Something wasn't right. He remembered them, and they weren't new. They were grubby and run-down. He was lost in his thoughts when the young woman broke through.

'Listen, could you help? This lady's lost a bangle. Looks like a snake.'

'Two cobras,' added Lal, in case that would help.

'Quiver,' said Anthony automatically.

'What?'

'It's a quiver of cobras,' explained Anthony. A crow sitting on a nearby telegraph pole squawked and caught Anthony's attention. 'A murder of crows'. An old lady trotted past with a Pekinese dog on a short lead. 'A pomp of Pekinese.' The facts came tumbling out of Anthony seemingly at random.

Lal and the young woman exchanged concerned looks. Both considered the fact that Anthony was not quite right in the head. Anthony noticed the looks on their faces.

'I'm sorry,' he said. 'That doesn't really help, does it?' He refocused. 'A bangle, you say. Like a cobra.'

'Two cobras,' corrected Lal.

'Yeah, well, we was wondering if that was it,' added the young woman, pointing to the glinting metallic object in the drain. 'Our arms aren't long enough to reach.'

Anthony nodded. He peered down into the drain and saw the glint. It didn't cross his mind not to help, even though helping involved reaching down into the grubby drain. He took off his heavy overcoat and removed the fingerless glove from his right hand. Then he knelt down on the kerb and flexed his fingers as if he was a magician about to perform a coin trick. He slid his hand in between the narrow opening in the grate and stretched down as far as he could.

His head was turned to one side and he was looking at the toddler sitting in his buggy. The boy ignored him. He was much more interested in pulling at one of the shopping bags hanging behind him.

Anthony stretched down just a little bit more and managed to hook the tip of his middle finger around the metal object. It was curved and smooth; could be a bangle.

'Got it!' exclaimed Anthony as he pulled it up. Lal and the young woman looked on expectantly as Anthony withdrew his arm. Lal's face dropped when Anthony's hand came out and she saw that he was holding a pair of scissors.

'Not a bangle,' said Anthony. 'Sorry. Invented by Leonardo da Vinci, you know,' he added, indicating the scissors. 'Do you want them?'

Lal and the young woman both shook their heads no, and Anthony let them drop once again.

'Well, thank you for trying,' said Lal, and she held out a hand to help him up. Anthony's ungloved hand took hers, and as skin touched skin Anthony reacted immediately. He drew in a sharp breath. A shock wave tore through him. Energy coursed up his arm at lightning speed and exploded in the centre of his head. He was blinded by bursts of colour: oranges and reds and purples and whites. Then images started to bombard him. It was like a dream. There was no discernible beginning. He was just there. *There* was a wedding in India. There were mirrored shamiana tents, and garlands of flowers strung everywhere. It was the early fifties. There was nothing specific that Anthony could point at as an example of this, but, just as in a dream, he understood without understanding how.

The bride was sitting in her wedding chair, wearing an exquisite red sari. The floor around her was festooned with a sea of orange carnations. She lifted her head. It was Lal, and she was just sixteen. She smiled up at her husband. His name was Meher and he was a handsome young man, though some ten years her senior. He looked more nervous than she as he presented her with an ornately carved box. He lifted the lid and showed her the contents. Lal liked what she saw and reached in, pulling out her gold cobra bangle. She slid it on to her delicate wrist . . .

Without warning, the colours drained away like paintbrushes being washed clean and Anthony found himself looking at Meher and Lal standing in a rundown street in Manchester. Everything was blue-grey. All the life and joy of India had gone. They were outside Lal's tiny terraced house. A gaggle of braying skinheads was coming along the road. They hurled abuse and bottles at Meher and Lal. Meher hurried to open the front door while Lal clutched the cobra bangle on her wrist. Somehow Anthony understood that it gave her strength. She glared at the jeering skinheads as they passed. Meher had to pull his headstrong young wife into the house. He closed the door behind them, locking out the harsh and unfriendly world.

Lal opened the back door and stepped out into a wilderness. The small garden was hugely overgrown and unloved. Meher sneered. Just one more thing to hate about this place, but Anthony could tell that Lal had just fallen in love. She saw the potential . . .

Then, as if time was surging forward, Anthony saw the garden changing. First it was cut down and tidied, then Lal and Meher planted. The seeds grew and the garden transformed into a truly magical place, where narrow pathways traversed bushes and rockeries from which a pantheon of statues of Hindu gods gazed out into the light . . .

Seasons came and went. Meher and Lal grew old together, until Anthony didn't see Meher any longer and he understood that he had died and Lal was alone. She was an old lady now.

He saw her standing in her living room, gazing at a

framed photograph of her wedding day all those decades before. She kissed the face of her husband and put the photo down. She took off the cobra bangle and laid it down on the arm of her chair. She rubbed her plump aching wrist. Then she turned off the light and headed up to bed.

Anthony stood in the darkness. Everything was quiet. Then a beam of light shone in through the window. It bounced off the TV screen and the stereo. It flitted around the room like some crazed firefly until it brushed over the bangle on the chair. It came back and the bangle glittered in the glare of the torch beam. Anthony turned and saw the face of a young boy at the window. Goose. He jimmied the lock with ease and came in to snatch up the bangle. He examined it in the light of his torch. Anthony watched him. He could see he was captivated by it. Then there was a noise from upstairs and Goose hurried away, leaving the way he came . . .

Lal shook loose of Anthony's hand and severed the link. Only a few seconds had passed and understandably the overload of information took its toll on Anthony. His knees buckled beneath him and he slumped to the ground, falling on all fours, breathing heavily. His head was pounding. The tendons at the base of his skull felt as if they were twisted tight like an old dishcloth. Flashes of light peppered the periphery of his vision. Lal and the young woman looked down at him with concern.

'Are you all right?' asked Lal.

It took several long moments for Anthony to catch his breath. The throbbing in his skull eased slowly. He tried to make sense of what he had seen.

'Your husband,' Anthony panted. 'He gave you the bangle.'

'Yes.' Lal sounded more than a little surprised.

'On your wedding day.'

Now Lal was starting to feel alarmed. 'How could you know that?'

Anthony shook his head. He had no idea. He didn't know this woman. He'd never seen her before in his life.

'I don't know,' he wheezed. 'I saw . . . your garden . . . India . . . A boy.'

'Boy? What boy?' asked Lal.

'He was at the window. He broke in. He took the bangle.'

The two women both looked distressed, but Anthony was even more so. He scrambled to his feet.

'I've got to go,' he said. There wasn't anywhere he wanted to go, but he knew he had to be somewhere else. Anywhere else.

'Wait,' pleaded Lal as Anthony hurried away, but he didn't hear her. He was scared. His head was buzzing now the pain had subsided. What was happening to him? First he couldn't remember how he got here. Now he was seeing crazy elaborate visions. That wasn't normal. He wasn't normal. He didn't know what *normal* was, but he knew he wasn't it. Was he going insane? Maybe he already was insane. Was he even here? Maybe he was walled up in an asylum somewhere and this was all a drug-induced hallucination. If it was, he wished he could hallucinate somewhere warmer. He hated being cold.

# 8

# HIPPOPOTOMONSTROSES-QUIPPEDALIOPHOBIA IS THE FEAR OF LONG WORDS

Goose was running as fast as he could, faster than he should. He kept hitting patches of ice hidden under the snow and his feet would skid out from under him, but he would keep going, stumbling, slipping, but always forward.

'MUTT!' Goose was scared now. Mutt never, ever ran away. Not once. Not even when he was a puppy. All Goose ever had to do was call him and Mutt would come running. Goose knew someone must have taken him. It was the only explanation. But who would take him and why? And, more importantly, where? '*MUTT!*'

Goose finally had to stop to catch his breath. He put his hands on his knees and gulped down great lungfuls of oxygen. Sweat poured off him, running down his face and dripping into the grey snow beneath him. He kept looking all around. The streets were busy. Half of Manchester seemed to be out doing last-minute Christmas shopping.

Suddenly he heard a bark somewhere in the distance. It was carried past him on the breeze. He stood up and looked around. Another bark. Still a long way off but from behind him. He spun round, looking along the street. He looked between the legs of thirty pedestrians in time to see something small and brown turning a corner.

'Mutt?' He started running again. He ran the two hundred metres to the corner, weaving between people, twisting and turning, always moving forward, always keeping his eyes on the corner.

When he got there he looked into the adjacent street. No sign of a dog. But then he heard another bark.

'MUTT!' he called. Another bark and he continued running. Down the street to the next corner. A crossroads. He looked in all directions. No dogs. Another bark and he took off running again, to his left.

\*

72

Anthony couldn't sit still. He was pacing back and forth, talking out loud. His only audience was a rather mangy-looking pigeon pecking at the remains of a bag of prawn-cocktail crisps that someone had tried to throw in a bin but missed.

'Something's happened,' Anthony told the bird. 'Happening,' he corrected himself, slumping down on a bench. 'I can't work out which bit's a dream and which bit's real. Or maybe none of it is . . .' With that he jumped back up on to his feet and resumed his pacing. 'Or perhaps I got knocked on the head.' He rubbed his gloved hands over his face and looked down at the pigeon. 'And now I'm talking to a pigeon.' Anthony stamped his foot in frustration, causing the bird to fly away.

'MUTT! HERE, BOY!'

Anthony turned in time to see Goose sprinting past. Instantly Anthony recognized him. He was the boy from the vision. The boy at the window. The thief.

Goose reached the middle of the park and stopped. He could see a long way in every direction and there was no sign of Mutt. Goose was ready to cry, but he sucked back the tears. He looked down and saw that his shoelace was untied. He focused on that, crouching down to tie it, forcing himself not to cry, willing the tears back into his tear ducts.

'Aglet!' Goose heard the word from behind him and

jumped up and spun round. He saw Anthony, who was frowning. Cross with himself because that wasn't the best way to start a conversation. Still, it was a way.

'You what?' asked Goose.

'Little hard bit at the end of your shoelace. It's called an aglet. And that . . .' Anthony pointed his finger at the gap between Goose's eyebrows. This was a bigger mistake. The attempt at physical contact put Goose on guard and he pulled back sharply. Anthony could see the wariness in the boy's eyes. He was thinking Anthony was a nutter at best, a perv at worst. He would get away from him as quickly as he could. Anthony knew he didn't have long to get Goose's attention. He knew he should just get to the point, but he was unable to. Some sort of mental block somewhere was stopping him. Making him talk. He wondered if he had Tourette's. Not that he shouted out swear words uncontrollably, but he assumed Tourette's came in many different shapes and sizes. 'That's your glabella.'

Goose was frowning deeply. Anthony persisted. 'It's true. You see, someone, somewhere has named everything. Think about it. *Everything!*' He emphasized the word. 'That's a lot. Not just one person, of course, that would be ridiculous. Did you know an owl has three eyelids? Bet you they all have a name.' In his head, Anthony was telling himself, *Get to the point! Get to the point!* but he seemed incapable of it. Despite himself, he just kept talking. 'You can make about eleven and a half omelettes from one ostrich egg, Coca Cola'd be green if they didn't add colouring and . . .' he took a deep breath, 'hippopotomonstrosesquippedaliophobia is the fear of long words.'

Anthony exhaled and finally stopped talking. Goose looked at him open-mouthed, buffeted by the torrent of trivia that this strange man had just unleashed.

'Is that true?' asked Goose.

'I'm not sure. I think so.'

'Fascinating!' Goose sneered, making it clear he wasn't fascinated or even interested and that he would very much like Anthony to go away. Goose started to walk past him but Anthony followed. Goose, however, was a tough kid. He had to be. He spent most of his time alone – well, with Mutt – and mostly out on the streets. He knew how to take care of himself or at the very least he knew how to project the idea that he knew how to take care of himself. In a year, no one had really tried to mess with him so he assumed it was working.

'Listen, I've tried to be nice, but I'm not interested, okay? So go and annoy someone else or I'm gonna start shouting at the top of me lungs! Got it?'

'Got it,' said Anthony.

Goose switched direction and started walking away. Anthony knew he only really had one more shot. It was all or nothing.

'So you lost something then?'

Goose froze, turning his head slowly to look back at Anthony. 'Yeah, how'd you know that?'

'What d'you lose?'

'My dog. He's called—'

Anthony held up his hand, closed his eyes and pinched the bridge of his nose as if concentrating hard.

'Mutt,' he said finally.

Goose actually gasped. He felt a flutter of excitement in his belly. 'Yeah! You seen him?' There was suddenly a childlike stutter of expectation in Goose's voice. Like something out of *Oliver Twist*.

'No, it's what you were shouting earlier.' Anthony could see the child in Goose retreat and the hard-edged mini-adult reappear. Silently he admonished himself. This was the wrong approach. He was losing him again. 'I lost a dog when I was about your age.'

'Is that right?' said Goose, wiping his nose on his sleeve. Anthony could sense Goose's invisible wall being rebuilt before his very eyes.

'Yeah, I think so. I mean I'm not sure. There's a lot I'm not sure about right now. Like this.' It was the only thing Anthony could think of to say at that precise moment. He grabbed the name badge pinned to his striped jacket and held it out to Goose. 'I don't feel like an "Anthony". Do I look like an "Anthony" to you?'

Goose frowned, and Anthony could tell he had hooked his interest once more. He was determined not to lose it again.

'Are you saying you don't know your own name?' Goose was looking for the angle, wondering if this weirdo was about to try to get some money off him.

'I don't want any money or anything,' said Anthony, apropos of nothing verbal.

'You what?' said Goose, wondering if Anthony was a mind-reader.

'You looked like you were thinking I wanted money off you,' said Anthony, by way of explanation.

'What does someone look like when they think that?' asked Goose, clearly incredulous.

'I don't know.' Anthony shrugged. 'Like you. Anyway, back to me not knowing my name.' *Don't lose his attention again*, Anthony told himself.

'How can you not know your own name?' asked Goose.

'I'm not sure. There seem to be lots of things I can't remember. Like I'm pretty sure I wasn't here yesterday, but today I am and I don't remember the bit in between. The getting here.'

'So where were you?' asked Goose.

'I don't remember. I remember lights. Lots of lights and noise.'

'Maybe you were abducted by aliens,' said Goose. 'I

saw a film about that once. People lose whole chunks of time.'

'It's a possibility, I suppose,' said Anthony. *Don't go off on a tangent!* He admonished himself in his head, partly because he already knew he was about to go off on a tangent. 'Did you know that the sun is three hundred and thirty thousand, three hundred and thirty times larger than the Earth?'

'Can't say I did know that,' said Goose. 'Or particularly want to know it,' he added.

*Get to the point! Get to the point!* 'And there are three hundred and thirty-six dimples on a regulation golf ball.'

Anthony could see Goose running the figures through his head.

Then the boy frowned. 'So? So what?' he asked. 'Three hundred and thirty thousand, three hundred and thirty, and three hundred and thirty-six aren't the same numbers.'

'No, but they're close.'

'No, they're not.'

'No, I suppose they're not. Similar though.'

Goose shook his head. 'They both have some threes in them. You seem to know a lot of useless facts.'

'Yeah, I do, don't I? Maybe I got hit on the head by an encyclopaedia salesman.' Anthony meant it to be funny, but he knew it wasn't, and he could tell Goose didn't think it was either. The boy was looking away.

'Look I've got to be going now, okay?' said Goose, having decided a direct and calm approach was probably the best way to handle this guy.

Anthony nodded. 'Okay.' *It's now or never*, he told himself.

'I don't want you following me. You tell me which way you want to go and I'll go the other way.' Goose sounded very reasonable and mature. Anthony suddenly felt like the child. 'You want to go that way –' Goose pointed west – 'and I'll go this way?' He pointed east. 'Or you go this way –' east – 'and I'll go that way.' West.

'By lying on your back and raising your legs, you can't sink in quicksand.'

Goose was already shaking his head before Anthony had even finished the sentence. 'That's not going to be much use in Manchester, is it? Not a lot of quicksand.'

'S'pose not,' muttered Anthony.

'And I don't want to know any more trivia,' added Goose.

'Dogs can make up to a hundred different expressions,' said Anthony hopefully.

'No,' said Goose, forcefully but still not losing his temper. 'Listen, Anthony, or whatever your name is, we need to go our separate ways now, okay?'

'But our paths must've crossed for a reason.'

Goose frowned. 'How d'you mean?'

79

'Well, it can't be a coincidence, can it?' asked Anthony.

'What can't?' Goose didn't understand.

'That I meet the boy who stole the bangle from the old lady right after I meet the old lady whose bangle you stole.' Anthony stopped to repeat that in his head to make sure it made sense. He was relieved that it did make sense and he had finally managed to say what he had been trying to say all along. Then he looked at Goose and could literally see the colour draining from his face. Anthony realized he had said the wrong thing. He was angry with himself. Goose started backing away.

'Don't go,' pleaded Anthony. 'There's some kind of pattern: she lost a bangle, you stole the bangle, you lost your dog and here we are. It's got to mean something, hasn't it?'

But Goose wasn't listening. He was scared. Who was this weirdo? How did he know about the bangle? Goose had to get away from him. As far away as possible. He turned on his heel and started running. Goose ran faster than he had all day. He looked back only once to make sure Anthony wasn't following. He wasn't. Goose kept going.

# 9

# WALKING ON EGGSHELLS

Helen Taylor woke softly as she felt a small body slipping into bed with her. She opened one eye and saw a lump making its way up towards her under the duvet. Then a small, perfectly formed little hand appeared and touched her face. Helen smiled.

'Hello, baby girl,' she whispered, and lifted up the duvet to see her daughter's beautiful, bewitching blue eyes smiling up at her from a face framed by a mass of blonde curls.

'Hello, Mummy,' said Milly Taylor. Helen kissed the palm of her six-year-old's hand and sighed.

Just then Helen became conscious of the sound of running water. She frowned and glanced over her shoulder, to see an empty space next to her where her husband should have been.

'What's your daddy doing up?' Helen asked Milly. The door to the en suite opened and Henry strode out. He was wearing a shirt and tie. Helen sat up, adjusting the pillow behind her. She realized that Milly wasn't in the bed with her any more. She hadn't noticed her leave.

'What are you doing?' she asked Henry.

'That's an odd question,' was his reply.

'Are you going to work?'

'Yes,' he said, but didn't look at her. He sat at the end of the bed with his back to her and pulled on his socks.

Helen was tall and thin. Bony, most would say. She had hard, angular features that were all perfectly in proportion, but there was nothing feminine about her. Her hands were large, the same size as a man's but with long, slender fingers. She was a strong, intelligent woman who had been to very good schools and paid attention. Both physically and intellectually she was intimidating and she knew it.

'Today?' She knew her tone was verging on combative but she didn't care. He couldn't possibly be going to work. Not today of all days.

'There's someone I have to see before the holidays.' Henry still didn't look at her. He flicked imaginary dots of lint from his socks; anything so as not to look at her. He could feel her glaring at the back of his neck, making his neck feel hot. He wondered if it was turning red. She said nothing, which was worse, and finally he felt compelled to turn. He looked at her but only from the side. 'It won't take long,' he said calmly. 'An hour or two at the most.'

'Don't worry. Take all the time you need.' He hated it when she sounded like that. The words were reasonable, but the tone was aggressive. There was a sharpness to them, making it clear how offended she was.

'Don't be like that,' he said. He could feel the ever-present anger creeping into his voice now. He had to leave quickly before he said something he'd regret. 'I have responsibilities.' Immediately he wished he hadn't said that.

'And what about your responsibility to me?' Helen let a beat of silence hang for just the right amount of time before adding, 'To Milly?'

Pain shot through Henry at the mention of the name. He had hardly slept. He had lain awake most of the night, listening to Helen snore softly. At one point she had cried out in her sleep. Henry had turned to look at her, wondering if he should wake her. He could see she was dreaming and that the dream was upsetting. He had a pretty good idea what the dream was about. He would have wanted her to pull him out of it, if it was the other way round, but he didn't do anything. He just looked at her and listened to her whimpering sobs until they stopped.

Henry stood up and threw on a jacket. He wasn't particularly tall. He liked to think he was of average height, but he was a little shorter than his statuesque wife. His body was solid with very little fat. He had the physique of an athlete and the head of an accountant.

'If I'm running late, I'll text you and meet you there.' He moved around the bed, pausing to lean down to kiss his wife. Helen turned her head away. Henry just kissed her roughly on the top of the head and left.

Helen covered her face with her hands and silenced a sob that reverberated through her.

Out in the hallway, Henry heard her. He wished he could go back in and make everything right, but he knew he couldn't. He didn't have the strength and, even if he did, some things can't be fixed. No matter what he did, it would never, ever be right again. He took a deep breath and headed down the stairs.

As he took his overcoat down from the hooks by the front door he saw a small pile of envelopes on the doormat. Mostly bills and junk mail. Henry looked through them. He stopped when he found a pale blue envelope. He stared at it for a moment and then he strode into the kitchen, opened the bin and dropped it in without a second thought. He headed back out to the hallway, wrapped his scarf around his neck, picked up his briefcase and left.

*

Helen heard the front door closing. She leaned her head back and stared up at the ceiling. The duvet rippled and Milly was back in bed again. Helen peeled back the covers and the little girl smiled.

'Are you hungry?' Helen asked. Milly nodded. 'What do you fancy?'

'Eggy bread,' she said.

'Eggy bread it is,' replied her mother. She ran her long slender fingers through her hair, looped it behind her ears and climbed out of bed.


Milly was already in the kitchen when Helen entered. The little girl was sitting on one of the high stools by the breakfast bar and twisting from side to side. Helen looked at the detritus left over from the previous night's Thai takeaway.

'I suppose I had better clear up first. Make a little space.' She busied herself loading the dishwasher. She had meant to cook last night, but time had got away from her and in the end they ordered in.

'Why's Daddy like he is?' asked Milly.

'How do you mean?' asked Helen, but she knew exactly what Milly meant.

'He's so cross all the time now.' Milly stopped swinging and considered a thought. 'Is it because of me?'

Helen didn't answer immediately, but eventually she nodded. 'Yes,' she said.

'But you're not cross. You're just sad all the time.'

'Different people deal with things like this in their own way.'

She crossed to the pedal bin with a plate, ready to scrape off the remains of pad thai and king-prawn keang kiew wan, but as soon as she opened the bin she saw the pale blue envelope Henry had discarded. She put down the plate and retrieved it, ripping it open with her finger.

It was just a Christmas card with a cartoon of a fat reindeer on the front. She opened it up and read the simple inscription: 'Thinking of you. Love from Anna, Mark and the sprogs.'

Helen threw the envelope back in the bin and headed out of the kitchen into the hallway. There were two doors leading into the large L-shaped lounge. She crossed to a chest of drawers, which stood behind a baby-grand piano and opened the second drawer down. She retrieved a shoe box, opened it up and added the card to about twenty others. She looked around at the bare room. There was no tree, no decorations, nothing. No indication at all that it was Christmas Eve. Henry had cancelled Christmas. She remembered that line in *Robin Hood*, the one when the Sheriff of Nottingham, played by that actor who's in everything . . . she was terrible with names . . . cancelled

Christmas in a fit of pique. That's what Henry was like. The thought made her laugh.

'What's so funny?' Milly was sitting on the piano stool, swinging her bare feet back and forth.

Helen shook her head. 'Oh, it's nothing. Just . . . you loved Christmas.'

'I still do,' said Milly. 'I wish we had a tree this year.'

'Me too,' said Helen.

'Why don't you get one? Today.'

'It would upset your father,' said Helen.

'He doesn't seem to worry about upsetting you,' said Milly.

'Now that's not fair,' said Helen, frowning.

Milly slid off the stool and crossed to the door. She turned and looked at her mother. She shrugged. 'It's not me saying that,' she said. 'After all, I'm not even here.' And with that Milly faded away.

It was one year ago today that Milly had died. Helen spoke to her more and more frequently, and she always missed her when she left.

# 10

# THE MAN WHO
# MADE IT SNOW

Goose couldn't sit still. He would sit down for a second or two, then jump to his feet, striding back and forth on the far side of Frank's stained and scuffed coffee table. Frank was sprawled out on the sofa sipping from a can of Beck's, watching Goose's maniacal marching, feeling a little fatigued by the frenzied activity before him, as Goose described his encounter with the weirdo in the park.

'And then he goes,' said Goose, pausing for effect, '"She lost her bangle, you stole it and you lost your dog."' Goose looked at Frank, adding a little involuntary affirmative nod of the head, unconsciously telling Frank it was time for him to agree that what had happened was extraordinary and twisted. Frank took a sip of his lager and said nothing. Not the reaction Goose wanted. He gnawed at the inside of his cheek. 'So what do you think?'

Frank just scratched at the ginger stubble on his jawline. 'I don't know, Goose. There's a lot of strange people in the world.'

'You reckon he's some sort of undercover copper?'

Frank's brow knitted as he ran over everything Goose had just told him, wondering if he had missed something; namely the bit that suggested that the bloke hanging about in the park was the Old Bill. Frank shook his head.

'Be serious, Goose. Manchester's finest have got better things to do than hang about in cold parks talking to kids on Christmas Eve. They could get themselves arrested.'

At that, Goose plopped down on the sofa, threw his head back, looked up at the ceiling and huffed. Frank wasn't treating this with the importance it deserved. Frank could see the irritation writ large on Goose's face. He felt bad, but still had the embers of a hangover so had to force himself to care. All he could think of to say was, 'So he have a name, then?'

'Anthony,' answered Goose, then added quickly, 'though he said it wasn't.'

'Wasn't what?'

'His name.'

Frank closed his eyes and concentrated. He rubbed his eyes. This conversation was more than he could handle. 'I don't understand. Was it his name or not?'

Goose shrugged. 'He had a badge that said, "I'm Anthony. How—"'

'– can I help?' Frank interrupted, finishing the sentence for Goose.

'Yeah, that's right.' Now Goose had the same confused look on his face as Frank. 'How'd you know that?'

'Cos I met him,' said Frank. 'Last night. Near the Witches. I think he made it snow.'

'You what?'

Frank suddenly realized how daft that sounded. 'Maybe it was a coincidence.' Frank wanted to change the subject. Then he remembered something relevant. ''Ere, he had dog collars on.'

'He what?' asked Goose.

'Yeah. On his wrist. Three of them.'

'Are you winding me up?' asked Goose.

'No, swear. It was weird. He wasn't there one minute and then . . .' Frank's voice trailed off as he caught himself and heard what he was saying.

'So,' said Goose, 'are you saying he's got Mutt?'

'Nah. Just . . . I don't know. There was a bloke in

90

Brockley I remember, used to go out nicking people's dogs, then waited for the reward posters to go up so he could claim the money.'

With that, Goose shot to his feet, paused a moment, then sat back down. Then, back to his feet.

'We need to go and find him,' said Goose.

'What d'you mean, "we"?' Frank really didn't have any plans to leave the sofa today. *Miracle on 34th Street* was on in half an hour. The old version, with Edmund Gwenn and Natalie Wood when she was little, not the colour one with Dickie Attenborough.

'He might be a total nutjob, Frank,' said Goose.

'All the more reason to leave him well alone, I'd say.'

'But what if he's got Mutt?' asked Goose. The desperation and need in his voice were plain to hear. Frank tried to block them out. He flipped through different answers in his head. What could he say to avoid having to go out, trudge down to the park and confront a loony? While Frank was considering his response, Goose said the one thing Frank couldn't ignore. The one thing that meant Frank *had* to go with him.

'My dad would have come.'

Frank grated his teeth together and thought of a dozen choice swear words, each more inventive and angry than the one before, but he didn't say any of them out loud. Once he'd finished muttering them all to himself he couldn't do anything but grunt out a laugh and shake his head.

'You're a manipulative little git, Goose, you know that?'

Goose smiled, picked up Frank's tatty leather coat and held it out to him. Frank knew he wasn't going to get to see *Miracle on 34th Street* after all.

# 11

# BUTTERED CHRISTMAS CARDS

Henry Taylor worked for the Greater Manchester Probation Trust. Their headquarters were housed in an eyesore of a building in Old Trafford, about halfway between United's home ground and the cricket ground. His was just one desk out of forty-two in a vast open-plan office. However, Henry was the only person in the office that day. His desk (fourth row from the door, sixth along) stood out from all the others as it was the only one that bore no Yuletide additions. Some of his neighbours seemed to be competing to see who loved Christmas the most. The desk to his right had a small potted tree caked in baubles weighing down its little branches, a doll of Santa, eight reindeer whose noses all flashed, two snowmen and a garland of holly running around the table's edge. The desk to his left looked like an explosion in a tinsel factory. There was practically a canopy of tinsel of all colours and mistletoe. The woman who sat there, Audrey Toohey, a pleasant woman though with alarmingly distracting cankles, had a crush on Henry, which he did his best to pretend to be oblivious to. Henry didn't even know what a cankle was until he met Audrey. It turned out to be the ankle of heavily overweight people where there was no discernible slimming between calf and ankle, hence cankle.

Henry's desk, in contrast to all the others, was mostly clear. There were several folders stacked in his in and out trays positioned just so on one side of the desk, the telephone on the opposite side and a single Manila folder sitting in front of him with a Bic biro placed on top. Henry sat with his fingers spired, his mouth and nose resting on them. He listened to the *tick-tick-tick* of the office clock and glanced up at it every ten seconds or so. He was waiting for someone, and whoever that someone was, they were late.

Finally Henry grew tired of waiting and watching the clock. He opened the folder in front of him, revealing the details of one of his juvenile probationers: 'Richard M. Thornhill'. A dour-looking photograph of Goose stared up at him. Henry ran his finger down the page until he found the home phone number. He picked up the phone and dialled. It started ringing.

Across town, in Goose's kitchen, Nan was baking bread. She was white with flour. Great puffs of it filled the air. She heard a muffled ringing and paused to listen with a frown on her face. *Where was that ringing coming from?*

She followed the sound around the kitchen from the oven to the washing machine and finally to the fridge. As she opened the door, the ringing became louder and Nan saw the cordless phone standing in the door. She saw a carton of milk on the worktop and swapped the two over. As she closed the refrigerator door and turned her attention to the phone, it stopped ringing. Nan looked annoyed. She liked to get phone calls. She opened the fridge and put the phone back inside. Then she returned to her mixing bowl.

Back in Henry's office, he replaced the handset and sat with his thoughts for a few moments. He looked at his watch and then up at the office clock. Both said the same time. It was getting late. He made a decision and stood up, gathering Goose's file, sliding his biro into his jacket pocket and throwing his topcoat over his arm. He left the office.

Henry drove across town in silence. He tried listening to the radio, but the chattering voices annoyed him. Most things annoyed him now. At some traffic lights a man on a bicycle slipped in front of him and stopped. This annoyed him. When the lights turned green it took the man on the bicycle almost three seconds to get going. This annoyed him. The man on the bicycle was forced to pedal directly in front of Henry's Volvo because the cycle lane to the left was blocked ahead with road works. This annoyed him.

Henry parked his car across the road from Nan and Goose's house and got out. He looked around, not comfortable in this neighbourhood. Further along the road he saw gaggles of children playing happily in the snow. He glared at them as if to say, *I've seen you, and if you mess with my car I'll know who you are.* The thing was, not one of the children was paying any attention to either Henry or his rather dull car.

Henry crossed the road and rang the doorbell. He waited, though he started to fidget with impatience almost immediately. After several moments he was about to ring the bell again when he heard movement on the other side of the door and he could hear Nan shuffling towards him. The door opened and Nan poked her head out. She was covered in flour now and looked like a courtier from eighteenth-century France, with white make-up and a powdered wig.

'Yes, what do you want?' asked Nan.

'Mrs Thornhill? My name's Henry Taylor. I'm Richard's probation officer.'

Nan frowned, looking blank. She shook her head. 'There's no Richard here, dear. No.' And with that, Nan closed the door in Henry's face. He closed his eyes and growled under his breath. He rang the doorbell again.

A few moments later, Nan reappeared. She smiled politely, as if seeing him for the first time.

'Can I help you, dear?'

'Mrs Thornhill, I'm talking about Richard, your grandson. He missed his appointment this morning.'

Nan blinked several times as she considered what Henry had said. 'Richard?' she repeated softly and slowly. 'My grandson?' Then, as if a switch had been flicked, she smiled genuinely this time. 'Oh, you mean Goose. No one calls him Richard. He's not in, dear. Sorry.'

Nan started to close the door, but Henry held up a hand to stop her.

'Mrs Thornhill, this is serious. The rules of Rich–' He stopped himself. 'The rules of Goose's probation are very clear. He can't miss any of his appointments with me. If he does, he could find himself taken into detention again.'

Somehow the severity of Henry's tone more than the words he was saying registered with Nan. Her cheeks flushed and she felt her pulse racing.

'I suppose you had better come in,' she said. Henry nodded and entered. Nan closed the door after him.

*

97

Nan picked up some post from the doormat, mostly Christmas cards. Henry followed her into the kitchen, where it looked as if it had been snowing inside. Nan sat at the table in front of a breadboard with the ingredients needed for a cheese and peanut-butter sandwich.

'I was just about to make Goose a sandwich for his lunch,' said Nan. 'Do you want one?'

Henry took out his handkerchief and dusted the flour from a chair so that he could sit down. He shook his head.

'Er . . . No, thank you,' he said. 'So you're expecting Goose home soon then?'

'Well, he'll be back for his lunch,' said Nan. 'He's always back for his lunch.'

'But it's only a quarter past ten.'

'Oh, is it? That late?' Nan shook her head and buttered two slices of bread. Henry watched in surprise as she then proceeded to open the Christmas cards she had just received in the post, read them and then butter them. Henry considered pointing out what she was doing, but decided, somewhat wimpishly, to ignore it.

'Have you any idea where Goose might be, Mrs Thornhill?'

Nan let out a long sigh and shook her head. '"*Somewhere between the moon and here.*" That's what my mother always used to say. He went out with Mutt this morning. Had an appointment . . .' Nan lowered her voice to divulge a little secret, 'with his probation officer.'

'That's me, Mrs Thornhill. Remember? Goose didn't show up. That's why I'm here.'

Nan furrowed her brow as she concentrated especially hard, trying to force her failing mind to focus.

'Well, he's usually back for lunch. I was just doing him a sandwich.'

Henry's shoulders sagged. He knew he wouldn't get any help from Nan. She was incapable of giving it. 'Would you like to stay?' she asked.

Henry realized at that moment that he wasn't angry with this old woman. Which was unusual for him. He felt desperately sorry for her as she gestured to a buttered Christmas card.

'No, thank you,' he said kindly. 'I can't today. It's not a good day.'

Nan put down the butter knife and let her hands flop into her lap. Her great rheumy eyes, which were magnified by her glasses, were filled with melancholy.

'No, it's not, is it?' said Nan in little more than a whisper.

'You're not very well, are you, Mrs Thornhill?' Henry asked, trying to sound as compassionate as he could.

Nan shook her head. 'No, I don't think I am.'

'Have you seen anyone? Has anyone seen you?' But Nan didn't answer. She sat staring blankly into the space between them. 'It must be very hard looking after a boy like Goose.'

At the sound of Goose's name, Nan seemed to snap back into the moment and she smiled.

'He's a bit of a handful,' she said. 'But "*in time all flowers turn towards the sun*". That's what my mother used to say.

'Well, until then, I think we should be giving you a lot more help.' In his head Henry was already running through the myriad of forms he would need to fill out in order to place Goose with a foster family, if possible, or into care if not; find a residential home for Nan; put the dog into kennels. And that would only be the beginning. There was the house, the possessions. It was a thankless task. He knew from experience that no one involved would be pleased with the changes that were about to befall them. Even if it was for the best. When people were in the middle of it, they could rarely see that. Fortunately for them, he could. He could see the big picture and make the hard decisions. That was his job and he took pride in performing it efficiently. Henry paused. When he was a kid he had wanted to be an astronaut and fly to the moon. Now he took pride in being efficient at filling out bureaucratic paperwork. When had that change happened?

Henry shook such thoughts from his head and focused on the job ahead of him. He needed to start the ball rolling. Today. Now.

# 12

# THE HAPPY PRINCE

It was a ten-minute walk to the park, but they made it in seven. Even though his legs were long, Frank had to walk twice as fast as his usual amble to keep up with Goose, who would have sprinted all the way if he could. They came in from the Hazlett Road side, squeezing through a gap in the hedge there. The middle of the hedge had been hacked out to create a little den favoured by junkies. Syringes and twisted pieces of foil littered the ground, but other than that it was empty at the moment.

As they emerged into the park they stopped to scour the landscape around them. This was where Goose had spoken with Anthony earlier, but now there was no sign of him. Goose's heart sank. What if he had vanished? Moved on? Taken Mutt with him? What if he never found him? What if he never saw Mutt again? All these thoughts raged through his head, making it throb with anxiety.

'There he is,' said Frank. Goose turned quickly to look at Frank, followed his gaze and saw Anthony standing under an old Victorian bridge with frosted green brickwork walls. Only then did Goose realize he had been holding his breath. He exhaled and his heart went *bombom! bombom!* in his chest.

Frank and Goose crossed the damp patchy grass towards the canal. They saw Anthony watching them approach. He was absent-mindedly spinning the poker chip back and forth between his fingers, like a distracted conjurer.

'Leave this to me,' said Frank, with a metal edge to his voice. Goose had never heard him speak like that. A ripple of fear ran through him.

They had to cross the bridge and come down a steep set of steps that had been chopped into the embankment there. The bridge itself was jewelled with icicles, dripping down from the tiled voussoirs. The green of the tiles stimulated a memory embedded deep in Goose's mind and he remembered a trip he took south with his parents years ago, when he was three or four. It was a place called Saltdean and there was an old outdoor swimming pool called the Saltdean Lido. This bridge was the exact same shade of green as the tiles at the bottom of that pool. Goose realized it was a strange thing to think about at that precise moment. He remembered his dad throwing him up into the air. He remembered his own weightlessness as he threw his little arms back and closed his eyes. He remembered time slowing down as he fell through the air and crashed into the water. He remembered sinking down and down and down, but he wasn't scared. He remembered opening his eyes and looking up, seeing blue sky above and his father's distorted face smiling down at him. His arms reached up and he pulled at the water, starting to rise, and as he broke the surface he was suddenly back in Manchester, in a park, on Christmas Eve, under a frosted green bridge and looking at a man who might or might not be called Anthony.

Frank stepped towards Anthony. Frank was the taller of the two, but Anthony looked the more solid. Frank used his height to try to intimidate, but Anthony didn't seem to notice. He had a blank smile on his face. Frank had the same hard edge to his voice when he spoke.

'Need a word, fella,' he growled.

Anthony breathed in, thinking, and then said, 'Floccinaucinihilipilification. There's a word. Long word. Twenty-nine letters. One more than antidisestablishment-arianism.'

This response took the wind out of Frank's previously aggressive sails.

'He does that,' said Goose. 'Should have warned you.'

'Have you seen an angel with a monkey's head anywhere around here?' Anthony asked, seemingly a genuine enquiry.

This further flummoxed Frank. He opened his mouth, left it open for a moment and then closed it again. The fight had gone out of him. He turned to Goose and shook his head. 'I think we should go. He's clearly a nutter.' Then, suddenly remembering Anthony was right next to him, he winced and smiled apologetically. 'No offence.'

Anthony shrugged. 'None taken. I can see how you might think that. Thought had crossed my mind. I was saying something similar to a pigeon earlier. That sounds odd now I say it out loud.'

'Who are you?' asked Frank, his head spinning.

'Now that's a question and a half,' said Anthony. Then he reconsidered and shook his head. 'Well, no, I suppose "What's the capital of Peru and how does a duck . . . ?" is a question and a half.'

'We should definitely go,' said Frank, already edging away.

Goose could see he would have to take charge. He stepped forward, rising to his full height of four foot five (he was small for his age) and puffed out his chest. 'What have you done with my dog?' he demanded.

'I haven't done anything with your dog,' said Anthony.

'So what's on your wrist?' Goose looked down at the three dog collars Anthony wore on his left wrist. Anthony lifted his arm and looked at them. He and Goose had the exact same quizzical look on their faces as they regarded them. Anthony struggled to remember the significance of the collars. His brow knitted. 'You nick dogs, don'tcha?' said Goose.

'Why would I do that?' asked Anthony, genuinely interested in the reply.

'For the reward!'

'Is there a reward?'

'NO! Gimme my dog back!' Goose was shaking with anger now. His fists were clenched and he was breathing heavily through his nose.

'I haven't got your dog,' said Anthony calmly.

Frank looked at Goose squaring up against the much bigger Anthony and decided he had to say something before things got out of hand. 'How did you know about the bangle?' he asked.

Anthony looked at him and considered his answer before speaking. 'I don't think you'd believe me. I'm not sure I believe me yet.'

Frank looked at Goose, and Goose looked back. Neither knew what that meant. Goose turned back to Anthony.

'Try us,' he said.

Anthony replied a dozen times in his head, trying out

a variety of ways in which to answer, looking for one that didn't sound too crazy. There wasn't one. 'I saw you take it,' he said out loud finally.

'No, you never!' Goose snapped back. Then he caught himself and played the words over in his head. That wasn't an admission of guilt, he told himself. He could have meant Anthony couldn't have seen him steal the bangle because he hadn't stolen it. Was never in that house. In fact, doesn't even know which house they're talking about. Anyway, he was somewhere else entirely when it was happening. Whenever that was.

'It's the truth,' said Anthony, as much to himself as to Goose and Frank. He looked at his own hand. 'It was an old Indian lady. I touched her hand and I saw . . . so many things. I saw her whole life. I saw her grow old. I watched her marriage in another country, in another time. I saw her husband give her the bangle. He died. Which made it all the more precious to her.' Anthony looked up from his hand to Goose. 'I saw you at her window with a torch. You jimmied the door from the garden. It was sitting on the arm of the chair. Two cobras in a circle. You took it and left.'

When he had finished, Frank and Goose said nothing. Goose could feel Frank's eyes boring into the side of his head, but he couldn't meet his gaze.

Finally Frank looked away from Goose and to Anthony. 'Just so I have this straight,' he said, 'you touched her hand and "saw" all this?' He made sweeping quotation marks in the air around the word 'saw'. 'Like in a vision or something?'

'Something,' Anthony agreed.

'This sort of thing happen a lot?' asked Frank, trying to be helpful.

'I don't think so.' Anthony's face darkened. 'And I think I'd remember. It hurt.'

'Hurt?' asked Frank.

Anthony nodded. 'A lot. Like burning needles slicing through my brain.'

'Eeurrgghh,' said Frank.

'Like rats scratching to get out of me from the inside. Biting.'

'Yeah, awright. We get it,' said Frank, who was actually quite squeamish. 'Sounds nasty.'

Sounds nasty? Goose looked at Frank with a deep sneer etched on his face. It sounded to him like Frank believed this rubbish. 'Oh, come on, Frank. You're not actually buying any of this old guff, are ya?'

Frank resembled a rabbit caught in headlights. He hadn't really got as far as considering whether or not he believed Anthony. He'd been reacting more to the images that his words threw up in his head. 'Well, I mean, I'm—' was about all Frank managed to say.

Goose was in no mood to entertain any of this as

potentially true. He was on the offensive straight away. 'So you expect us to believe that you touched this old woman's hand and saw me robbing her? said Goose, really pushing the incredulity in his voice. 'When that never happened. You know that'd never stand up in court, right?'

'I wasn't planning to go to court,' said Anthony.

But Goose wasn't listening. He was on a roll. 'So come on then, show us this amazing mind-reading gift, Derren-sodding-Brown. Frank, give him your hand.'

'What?' said Frank, suddenly scared.

'I'd rather not,' said Anthony quietly, though Goose wouldn't have heard him whatever the volume.

'Give him your hand, Frank. Let him tell you what you've lost. Old lady's lost a bangle; he knows I've lost a dog. Well, you've lost something too. Let him tell you what.'

'I don't want to,' said Anthony, more forcefully this time. Goose heard the words but still was choosing to ignore them.

'Course you don't. Cos it's a load of old bolsh.'

'It hurts,' said Anthony meekly, remembering the sensation and not relishing it.

'Yeah, yeah, needles and rats,' sneered Goose. 'We get it.' Goose was so worked up that he had pushed towards Anthony, getting closer and closer.

Anthony responded to his increasing proximity by moving back until now he was pressed up against the green-tiled abutment with nowhere left to go. Suddenly Goose's hands shot out from his body. He grabbed hold of Anthony's sleeve with one hand and Frank's with the other. He slapped their two hands together, too fast for either man to react. And as skin touched skin Anthony drew in a sharp breath. He felt a sensation like pins and needles times a thousand coursing up his arm. The feeling spread quickly through his body: flooding into his chest, rising up through his throat, into his head until it reached the very centre of his brain.

The bridge and canal and park vanished and Anthony found himself in Frank's grotty flat, standing behind the sofa, looking down at Frank slobbed out beneath him. Frank was drinking from a can of lager, king-prawn bhuna in a foil takeout container resting on his chest, staring through heavy-lidded eyes at *Antiques Roadshow* on the television in front of him.

On-screen a book expert wearing a pair of white gloves, like a snooker referee, was holding a small maroon-coloured hardback in his hands, rotating it slowly, reverentially opening the pages and breathing in its musty, hundred-year-plus odour. A woman in her late eighties with a neat white bob was sitting across from him, listening intently to what he had to say. Frank watched, sucking up a prawn as he did, sauce dribbling down his chin.

'What we have here,' said the expert, 'is a very early

edition of Oscar Wilde's *The Happy Prince*. I remember reading this as a boy. It's a marvellous story.'

'My father bought it for sixpence during the war,' said the old woman with the neat white bob.

'Sixpence,' said the book expert with a patient smile in his voice.

'It was a lot of money then,' added the old woman. 'For us, anyway. We were very poor. We lived in Coventry. Lost everything in the Blitz in forty—'

But the book expert didn't want to hear her life story. He was more interested in the small, thin book, which he now lay on the table in front of him. He put his hands together as if he was about to start praying, resting the tips of his index fingers on his chin.

'Wilde published *The Happy Prince* in 1888 in a collection of short stories. This edition was released by Raven Publishing some seven years later. So not a first edition, but interestingly Raven Publishing didn't exist for very long, and the illustrator they commissioned for their Wilde series was Arthur Rackham, quite early in his career. He had only been illustrating for about two years when he worked on this. Sadly Raven went bankrupt almost immediately afterwards.'

'Oh dear,' said the sweet little old lady, but what she really meant was *howmuchhowmuchhowmuch?*

'You probably want to know how much this is worth

today,' said the book expert, nodding knowingly. They all just want to know how much. 'This is in reasonable condition, a little wear and tear on the spine but nothing too serious. I would think this could fetch somewhere in the region of . . .' He paused for maximum effect. The old woman with the neat white bob was hanging on his every word. So too was Frank. '. . . Forty thousand pounds.'

The old woman was looking at the book expert open-mouthed. Frank was staring at the TV screen open-mouthed. Then suddenly he leaped to his feet. His king-prawn bhuna landed face down on the carpet with a splat! Frank hurried over to the packing boxes lined up against the wall and started riffling through them one at a time. He dumped the contents of each on the floor around him, clearly looking for something specific.

Back in the park, Anthony let go of Frank's hand and slumped back against the green wall. His whole body was shuddering from the experience of seeing inside someone else's head. His face was a light beige colour and a film of greasy sweat clung to him. He pushed the heels of his hands into his eye sockets in an attempt to alleviate the drilling in his brain. The shaking eased off after a few moments and he caught his breath. The pounding in his head eased off too.

111

'Was that it? That were impressive. So?' asked Goose, eager to prove Anthony a fraud.

Anthony took several deep breaths and the colour started to return to his face. 'A book.'

Both Goose and Frank were unable to hide their astonishment.

'What book?' Goose was cross. This was not the answer he had expected.

'*The Happy Prince* by Oscar Wilde,' said Anthony. He could see from the looks on their faces that he was right, but he knew that already.

Frank started to laugh, which made Goose even angrier. 'Bloody hell!' said Frank. 'Bloody hell!' he said again. Then he looked straight at Anthony, desperation on his face. 'Do you know where it is? I've been looking everywhere for that.'

Anthony shook his head. 'Sorry. I didn't stay long enough to see that.'

'So do it again,' pleaded Frank, thrusting out his hand. 'Please!'

Anthony looked at Frank's outstretched hand as if it was a red-hot poker he was being asked to hold by the glowing end. But it might well have been. A poker probably would have hurt less.

'It's a wind-up, Frank!' said Goose. He turned on Anthony. 'Tell him! Tell him how you know. You could've asked someone.' He alternated his focus between Frank and Anthony. 'People know you've been looking for it. You've asked around. Someone told you, that's all.'

'No,' said Frank, shaking his head. 'No one told him. He saw it just like he said.' Frank emphasized his hand, which was still outstretched. 'Please.'

Anthony stared at Frank's hand. The last thing in the world he wanted to do was take hold of it, but he knew he was going to. He summoned up the courage from within and slowly he put his hand out. It hovered just over Frank's. The last few centimetres were the hardest. Scared Anthony might change his mind. Frank grabbed his hand and held on to him tightly. Anthony reacted immediately. He drew in a sharp breath and then a violent jolt rippled through him. Then another. His eyes grew wide and his mouth opened to scream but no sound came out. Then he started shaking as if gripped by palsy. His eyes rolled back so only white was showing. He emitted a strangled gurgle and his legs buckled beneath him as he dissolved into a heap on the ground. Frank let go as he fell away. Anthony hit the ground with a resounding thud and didn't move. Goose and Frank stood over his inert form.

'Bloody hell, Frank. I think you've killed him,' said Goose.

Frank crouched down and was about to pat Anthony's

113

cheeks because he'd seen that in a film once, when Goose stopped him. 'I'm not sure you should touch him again.'

Frank froze, realizing that Goose was right. Instead, he leaned over him. 'Anthony? Can you hear me? Anthony?' After a moment, Anthony groaned and Frank breathed a sigh of relief. 'Oh thank God, he's not dead. Anthony? Wake up.'

Anthony's eyelids fluttered open and it took him a moment to focus on Frank and Goose. Frank helped him to sit up, making sure only to touch his clothing. He sat him back against the wall and tried to control the eagerness apparent in his voice. 'What happened? What did you see?'

Anthony said nothing for several long seconds. His mouth was dry.

'Did you see it?' asked Frank. 'Do you know where it is?'

Anthony hesitated again before nodding his head ever so slightly.

'Tell me,' said Frank. And then more insistently, 'Tell me what you saw.'

# 13

# WHAT ANTHONY SAW
# INSIDE FRANK'S HEAD . . .

The first thing Anthony saw was a younger, happier Frank. He was lying on a wide bed with his wife, Alice. Anthony looked around at the room. It was clear they didn't have very much money, but what they did have had been spent well. They had made a little go a long way. There was a sparkle to everything in the room, as if he was seeing a rose-tinted memory. Alice was heavily pregnant, about ready to pop, and Frank had his head next to her belly, reading to their unborn child. He was reading from *The Happy Prince*.

'"High above the city, on a tall column, stood the statue of the Happy Prince. He was gilded all over with thin leaves of fine gold, for eyes he had two bright sapphires, and a large red ruby glowed on his sword-hilt . . ."'

Alice looked down at Frank and stroked his mane of thick hair as he read. A deeply contented smile played on her lips. The same smile was mirrored on Anthony's lips . . .

In the blink of an eye the location changed and Anthony found himself sitting on a small rocking horse in a child's bedroom. A pink lampshade with embroidered princesses hung from the ceiling directly above him. There were garlands of pink paper flowers running along the picture rail and criss-crossing the magnolia walls. It was a very girly room.

Anthony glanced over to the bed and he saw Frank again. Just a little older than before. His three-year-old daughter, Jemma, was curled up in his arms as he read to her from the same book.

'"He was very much admired indeed. 'He is as beautiful as a weathercock,' remarked one of the Town Councillors . . ."'

Frank's voice had the exact same timbre as when he had read to Alice's belly. And, as if the little girl could remember, she had a serene look of contentment on her face.

Alice stood in the doorway watching without being seen, and smiling just as she had before. She watched her husband, whom she loved very dearly, and their beautiful little girl, who had long, straight blonde hair just like the embroidered princesses on her lampshade.

Anthony craned his leg over the head of the rocking horse as he clambered off clumsily, but he was just a ghost and no one was aware of his presence . . .

Everything changed just as suddenly as before. Now Anthony was standing in the middle of a long, narrow hallway. Gone was the sparkle and the warmth. It had been replaced by a chill in the air.

Anthony looked to the stairs and saw Alice sitting on the bottom step with her arms wrapped around her legs. Tears were streaking her cheeks; her eyes were red and puffy.

'Bloody Australia!' Anthony heard this from behind him and he turned to the front door. There was no one there. The top half of the door was frosted glass, but there didn't seem to be anyone outside. Then Anthony noticed the letter box in the middle of the door and he saw Frank, or at least his eyes, framed within it. 'How do you bloody well expect me to react, Alice? It's the other side of the bloody world!' He spat the angry words.

Alice held herself tighter and choked back the tears to speak. 'Please, Frank.' Anthony could hear the desperation in her voice. This was a woman at the end of her tether. 'I can't do this any more.' She was begging. There was a long pause and then she added, 'It's all gone so wrong since . . .' But she didn't finish the sentence.

Anthony looked back to the letter box, waiting for Frank's frenzied reaction, but when he spoke his voice was quieter, as if the fight had been knocked out of him with that half-sentence. 'You're saying it was my fault?'

Alice looked up sharply, shaking her head just a little. Frank had misunderstood and her first instinct was to correct him, but her second instinct said maybe it would be easier if she didn't and that's the one she listened to.

'You're just the same as all the rest,' said Frank, defeated. The letter box snapped shut and Anthony watched as his silhouette rose up and walked away. Huge sobs reverberated through Alice as she couldn't hold back the dam any longer. Anthony saw movement out of the corner of his eye and looked up the stairs to see Jemma come running down to comfort her mother. Jemma was now nearly eleven. She cuddled into Alice. Mother and daughter both crying . . .

Without warning, Anthony found himself looking at a brick wall. He turned around to find himself back in Frank's flat. The door opened and Frank entered carrying two bags full of bottles. He threw his leather coat down and slumped on to the sofa, where he sat motionless for several long moments. Anthony walked around to stand in front of him, but of course Frank didn't notice. Frank wiped his eyes roughly and turned his attention to his bags. He started to unpack them, lining up a bottle of vodka, followed by a bottle of bourbon, another bottle of vodka, two bottles of wine, several bottles of lager and another bottle of bourbon.

Then he stood and strode into the kitchen. He returned with two glasses – a tumbler and a wine glass – and set them on the table. He opened a bottle of wine first, screw top, and poured a large measure. Anthony understood that Frank planned to drink everything in front of him and he wasn't sure if he would be here in the morning. He watched Frank take the first sip. He drained half the glass. Anthony reached out his hand to stop Frank as he raised the glass again, but Frank's arm just passed through Anthony as if he wasn't there, which of course he wasn't. The glass was now empty and Frank refilled it.

Frank leaned back, staring vacantly into space, mechanically raising the glass to his lips and drinking. His demeanour made Anthony think of a factory worker performing some repetitive and mindless task. Frank closed his eyes tightly, blocking tears and memories. He opened his eyes again and was about to take another sip when something caught his attention. He tilted his head to the side, staring across the room at one of the many boxes stacked against the wall. He put his glass down and clambered to his feet, already a little unsteady as the wine started to take effect. He lurched towards the box and lifted one flap, revealing a book that had been poking out. It was *The Happy Prince*. He opened it up and flicked through the pages. Slowly he started to drift back to the sofa. He sat back down and turned to page one. Tears mushroomed in the corners of his eyes as he read the first line: 'High above the city, on a tall column, stood the statue of the Happy Prince . . .'

Another sudden change and Anthony found himself in the Witches later that same night. The pub was heaving. Anthony looked around and saw Frank sitting at a small table in the corner. He was drinking pints with whisky chasers, and he was still reading the book. Anthony sat at the only other chair at his table, and as he did so, Frank stopped reading, put the book down and looked up, straight at Anthony.

'Can you see me?' asked Anthony. Frank didn't respond and Anthony had his answer. Frank got to his feet gingerly and pulled on his long leather coat. He fumbled to put the book into his pocket and didn't notice as it dropped out. He kicked it across the floor as he staggered to the door.

'Ni', Mick,' he called to the landlord as he tumbled off into the dark.

Anthony looked down at the book sitting in the corner,

just as a wrinkled, liver-spotted hand reached down and picked it up. The hand belonged to a tall, irascible-looking man in his eighties. His name was Dr Rafe Clarence. He was a regular fixture in the Witches but rarely spoke with anyone. He had a battered old paperback of his own, some Second World War guts-and-glory potboiler. Dr Clarence was an insatiable bookworm. Read anything he could get his hands on. He put his well-thumbed paperback aside and was flicking through *The Happy Prince* as Mick appeared at his table to collect glasses.

'Same again, Dr Clarence?' asked Mick, gesturing with his chin to the empty pint glass in front of the doctor.

'No, that's my lot for the night. Mind if I borrow this?' he asked, holding up Frank's book.

Mick frowned as he looked at it and shook his head. 'Not mine. Someone must have left it in here. Keep it.' Mick walked away, continuing his hunt for errant empties, and Dr Clarence considered his new acquisition. Then he stood, put on his coat, put both books into his pockets and headed out into the cold.

Anthony watched him go. He had his answer.

Back in the park, Anthony finished his description of what he had seen and Frank was lost for words. Though not for long.

'Dr Clarence. My God! Of course. Man's always

reading. Reads like a book a day, sometimes two, he told me once. I can't believe it. This is amazing.' Frank couldn't stay still. His mind was racing.

Goose could see Frank's excitement, but he wasn't convinced. 'Aw, come off it, Frank. He touches your hand for, like, a millionth of a second and can tell you something *you* couldn't possibly know. How could he learn that from you if you didn't know it to begin with?'

Frank looked blank and shrugged. 'I don't know.' He turned to Anthony, who looked just as blank and also shrugged. 'I don't know either,' he said.

Goose let out a howl of exasperation. 'I don't have time for this. I need to find Mutt. Please, Frank . . .' Goose looked imploringly at Frank, who shrugged awkwardly and shook his head.

'Sorry, Goose. I have to get that book. You understand.'

But Goose didn't understand. 'It's just a book,' he snapped. *Not a living, breathing thing like Mutt,* he thought.

'It's not about the book. It's about Jemma and Alice. I'm going to lose them and I can't let that happen. If I get the book, it means I don't lose them.'

Goose still didn't understand how a book could stop Frank's wife and daughter from emigrating to the other side of the world, but there was a determination to Frank that Goose hadn't seen before.

Frank shook his head. 'I can't lose them, Goose. I just

122

can't. Sorry.' Frank couldn't look Goose in the eye. He backed off a little and then turned and started to walk away. Goose opened his mouth to protest but couldn't think what to say.

Anthony stepped up in front of Goose. He shrugged. 'Perhaps it's all connected: book, bangle, dog. Find one; find them all.' Goose frowned: could that be true? 'You never know,' said Anthony, and he walked off too, after Frank.

Soon both men had disappeared up the embankment and over the bridge. Goose heard Anthony's footsteps echoing from above and then he was all alone. Now what?

# 14

# THE DOCTOR WHO HAD HIMSELF STRUCK OFF SO NO ONE WOULD BOTHER HIM

Frank marched ahead with purpose as Anthony and Goose followed behind. As they progressed, the neighbourhoods started to change and the houses became bigger and grander. They left behind the two-up, two-down new builds, moved through the 1930s semi-detacheds and approached the detached, four-storey Victorians with their gravelled fronts and high surrounding walls.

Frank had been surprised when he'd discovered where Dr Clarence lived. It had been a topic of conversation one night in the Witches. The surprise was because he lived nowhere near the pub. There were at least half a dozen pubs much closer to Dr Clarence's home and as Frank walked he remembered that he always suspected there were good reasons why none of those were his local. Dr Clarence was what was politely called a *'curmudgeon'* or less politely called a *'grumpy old git'*. Frank guessed he had made himself unpopular in each of those venues and now he had to trek the best part of an hour for a pint. Chances were that one day soon enough Dr Clarence would burn his bridges at the Witches too, and then he would be forced to walk even further.

Frank stopped outside Dr Clarence's large and imposing house and waited for Anthony and Goose to catch up.

'Bloody hell,' said Goose, looking up at the gothic red-brick monstrosity in front of them.

'Yeah, I know. It's a bit Addams Family,' said Frank.

'Who?' asked Goose genuinely. Frank shook his head as if to say, *Never mind.*

They stepped through a tall, wrought-iron gate that had been left ajar and crunched across the gravel drive to a set of steps leading up to a tatty enclosed porch. The wooden surround had once been painted green, but its hue had faded with time to more of a dirty grey. Its windows were stained-glass and were once probably beautiful, but through neglect they had become dull and lifeless under thick grime. Goose couldn't help thinking that a good wash would make them look a hundred times more inviting.

There was an ancient bell pull above a brass plate which read: 'Doctor R. Clarence', but someone had taken a hammer and chisel to the 'Doctor' and done their utmost to obliterate it. However, it was still just about legible. Frank pointed to the plaque.

'He had himself struck off,' he said, by way of explanation.

'Had himself struck off?' said Anthony, frowning.

Frank nodded. 'When he retired. Said if he stayed on the register and someone had a heart attack in the street he could get sued if he didn't treat them cos he was still officially a doctor. Not sure that's true, but they don't come much stubborner than Dr Clarence.'

'Then how come he's still called "Doctor"?' asked Goose. Frank thought about it, and from the look on his face probably for the first time. He didn't have an answer and shrugged. Then he pulled the knob and they heard the sound of a proper old bell clanging somewhere deep in the bowels of the house.

A few moments later they heard footsteps approaching and the inner door opened as someone entered the porch. They saw a turbid eye studying them through one of the few clear pieces of glass in the stained-glass door. Then they heard several chains and bolts being removed and pulled back and then the door opened. Dr Clarence stepped out and examined the three people on his doorstep with undisguised suspicion.

'Frank? To what do I owe this . . .' He left a deliberate pause before completing the sentence: '. . . visit?'

Frank smiled. 'Hello, Rafe. I was just wondering if you might have picked up a book I left in the Witches a while ago. *The Happy Prince.*'

Dr Clarence's frown deepened. 'Oscar Wilde? Would have thought *Nuts* was more your sort of thing, Frank.' Frank took the dig in good humour and smiled some more. 'I suppose you'd better come in,' said Dr Clarence, and he stepped aside.

Frank, Goose and Anthony walked past Dr Clarence, through the porch and into possibly the largest entrance hall Goose had ever seen. It was larger than any of the rooms in his nan's house. Almost larger than all of them put together. There was a black-and-white chequered tile floor leading to a wide curving staircase. There was a big round table directly in front of them, an ornate mirror to their right and a stunning grandfather clock to their left. But this wasn't the first thing a person would notice on entering. On the table, on shelves and in stacks around the edge of the hall were books. Thousands of books: hardbacks and paperbacks written by every author from Shakespeare to J. K. Rowling and everyone in between. Dr Clarence was more a hoarder than a collector. His house was overrun with them.

Frank looked a little overwhelmed by the sheer volume and disorganization before him. 'Bloody hell,' he muttered quietly to himself.

Dr Clarence closed the front door behind them and headed over to a door on their right. 'In here,' he ordered. Frank, Goose and Anthony duly followed.

They entered a large study-cum-drawing room. All available wall space was taken up with floor-to-ceiling mahogany bookshelves, and every shelf bowed in the middle under the weight of the books piled on to them. Books were stacked both vertically and horizontally. There were also short towers of books scattered all over the floor and piles on pieces of furniture and every available surface.

'You might have to make some space,' said Dr Clarence as he sat in a worn leather armchair: the one piece of furniture not drowning under literature. Anthony, Frank and Goose looked to a large green couch and had to remove several stacks of books before they could sit.

'So,' said Frank. 'About my book . . .'

'What about it?' asked Dr Clarence.

'Well, do you know where it is?' said Frank, gazing around at the thousands of novels surrounding him and suspecting that the answer was no.

'How do I know it's yours?' asked Dr Clarence.

Frank turned back to look at him, realizing that this might not be as straightforward as he had hoped.

'It's mine,' said Frank resolutely. 'I left it in the Witches. Take my word for it. Do you have it?'

Dr Clarence brought his hand to his chin and turned his head away. 'I'm thinking,' he said. 'I seem to remember it was an old edition. Illustrated by Arthur Rackham, if memory serves.' Frank gave a noncommittal nod. He was worried that he would give away the book's true value and then greed would get in the way. Frank had a very low opinion of pretty much everyone. 'Hmm, yes . . .' said Dr Clarence. 'Must be worth a pretty penny.'

'Forty thousand pounds,' said Anthony, suddenly remembering what the expert had said on the television.

Goose turned to look at Frank, his mouth agape. Had he heard right? 'Forty thousand pounds?' he exclaimed. He couldn't believe it. 'For a book?' He looked at the faces of the adults. It wasn't a joke.

Frank's eyes were closed and his fists clenched, digging his fingernails into the palms of his hands to stop himself from losing his temper.

129

'As much as that?' said Dr Clarence with a mischievous grin flickering on his lips.

Frank opened his eyes and forced a calm tone into his voice. 'Sentimental value,' said Frank. 'Used to read it to my daughter when she was little. Belonged to my dad. Been in my family a long time and I'd like it back, Rafe.'

'I'm sure you would,' said Dr Clarence, clearly enjoying toying with Frank. 'I'm curious. Why do you think *I* picked it up in the Witches?'

Frank and Goose both involuntarily glanced at Anthony. The look was not lost on Dr Clarence. He frowned.

'What? Why look at him?' He studied Anthony. 'I don't remember seeing you before.'

Finally Goose sighed and said, 'He touched Frank's hand and saw you pick it up. Like in a vision or something.'

Dr Clarence tittered for a second, then stopped abruptly as he saw from the looks on Frank and Anthony's faces that Goose was being serious.

'I know. Crazy, right?' said Goose.

Suddenly Anthony spoke: 'What sort of doctor are you?'

'I'm not,' said Dr Clarence. 'Any more,' he added. 'I was a GP.'

'Have you ever come across anything like this before?' asked Anthony.

'What? Someone having visions? Of course, they used

130

to be in my surgery all the time. Dozens of them. Hundreds.'
Dr Clarence smiled to himself.

'I'm serious,' said Anthony. 'It hurts, you see, when it happens.'

Dr Clarence stopped smiling, affected by Anthony's obvious sincerity. 'I'm sorry. No, I never heard of anything like that.'

'Would you examine me?' asked Anthony.

'No,' said Dr Clarence firmly. 'I'm not a doctor any more.'

'But it's not like you've forgotten everything,' said Anthony.

Goose scoffed: 'Why not? You have.' He smiled, pleased with his quick remark, but then he noticed no one else was smiling and felt self-conscious.

'What do you mean by that?' asked Dr Clarence.

'He's lost his memory,' said Frank, by way of explanation. 'Doesn't know who he is. Doesn't remember a thing.'

''Cept for bobbins about owls and aglets,' said Goose, finding it hard to keep the irritation out of his voice.

'Aglets?' asked Dr Clarence.

'The hard bit at the end of your shoelace,' said Anthony.

'Interesting,' muttered Dr Clarence, his mind elsewhere.

'No, it's not!' barked Goose, having swallowed his frustration long enough. He jumped to his feet. 'It's

131

mental. Why's it all about him? What about Frank's book? It's his, not yours, and you should give it back. And I know there's one place Mutt definitely isn't and that's here.'

'Mutt?' asked Dr Clarence.

'My dog! He disappeared and he –' said Goose, stabbing an angry finger in Anthony's direction – 'knows where he is.'

'Lost dogs, lost books. Good Lord,' said Dr Clarence.

'There you go,' said Anthony. 'That's what I said. There must be a connection. Lost bangles too. The bangle brought me to Goose, Goose brought me to Frank, Frank brought me to you.' He looked at Dr Clarence. 'What have you lost, Doctor?'

Dr Clarence shook his head. 'Me? Nothing.'

'Did you retire through choice or pressure?' Anthony asked.

'Very much my choice,' was Dr Clarence's reply.

Anthony's brow knitted as he thought. There was still so much fog in his head. So much of his past obscured. But it seemed as if he was here for a reason. He was almost sure of it. It was only a feeling, nothing he could articulate, but a voice in the back of his head was telling him he was on the right track. He came to a decision and removed his glove. He held out his hand to the doctor.

'I told you, I haven't lost anything,' said Dr Clarence.

'There's no need to worry. It only hurts me,' said Anthony.

Dr Clarence hesitated. He stared at Anthony's offered hand. The atmosphere was heavy with tension. Dr Clarence lifted his hand, started to reach out but stopped. He looked into Anthony's eyes and saw his reluctance – even though this was Anthony's decision, even though he was the one with his hand outstretched. Dr Clarence could see the anxiety in his face. It hurt, he had said. *This is not something he wants to do, but rather something he feels he has to do.* Dr Clarence was intrigued. He let his hand continue. He took hold of Anthony's hand. And as skin touched skin Anthony drew in a sharp breath.

This time the sensation was even more violent. It felt as if Anthony's arm was being clamped in solid metal. The feeling spread up, past his elbow, over his shoulder and then penetrated him, burrowing into his armpit, like the root of an iron tree frantically searching out sustenance. The wormlike root drilled into him, through his chest and then launched skywards, snaking up his throat until it reached the centre of his brain. Everything went black.

Anthony opened his eyes and found himself staring at a ceiling. He turned his head and discovered he was lying on a familiar black-and-white chequered tile floor. He sat up and he knew he was still in Dr Clarence's house. However, it was very different in one immediately apparent aspect: no books.

Anthony climbed to his feet. He looked around and saw the table and the grandfather clock, the ornate mirror and the curving staircase. Everything was clean and bright and loved. The table was highly polished and visible, not covered in a mountain of novels. Instead there was a vase in the centre of it, full of lilies. Sunlight shone through the stained glass in the porch, splashing pools of colour across the floor.

Then Anthony heard a ringing phone coming from the drawing room and he moved towards the sound . . .

The drawing room was as bright and joyous as the hallway. There were more flowers in here and the only books were neatly lined up on the shelves. Heavy velvet curtains were tied back and bright sunshine was streaming in. Anthony saw a trim phone chirruping on the desk and was just thinking that that was odd, seeing as the trim phone was a fixture in the 1970s but was mostly extinct nowadays, when the door behind him opened and Dr Clarence entered. He was forty years younger than the man Anthony knew. His hair was long, touching his collar, and he had thick, lustrous sideburns. As Dr Clarence answered the phone, Anthony crossed to the window and looked out. He saw a light blue

Vauxhall Viva parked in the driveway outside. A Hillman Imp drove past. He realized this was the seventies.

'Yes, hello,' said the younger Dr Clarence into the telephone. Anthony turned to look at him. 'Where the ruddy hell are you? I've been worried sick.' The doctor listened to the person on the other end of the phone and as he did so his face grew darker. 'What do you mean? When are you coming home? What does that mean? Where are you going?' He listened some more and his features grew more and more purple with rage until he exploded: 'Who are you with? I demand you come home right this second. You're my bloody wife, Emily, and you will do as you are ruddy well told!' He listened some more, his breathing heavy. 'Letter? What letter? In the kitchen? What are you talking about? Come back and talk to me face to face.' Then, as if realizing this was the wrong approach, he softened. 'We can work this out if only we could speak. Please come back. Emily? Emily . . . ?' As he realized his wife had hung up, his fury overtook him and he smashed the receiver back down on to the cradle with enough force to shatter the phone. Then he turned and pounded out of the room . . .

Anthony was already in the large, bright kitchen. He was looking down at an envelope addressed to 'Rafe' sitting on the table propped up against the toast rack.

The door crashed open as the younger Dr Clarence stormed in. A breeze dislodged the letter and Anthony watched helplessly as it skimmed off the table and floated down to the floor where, unbelievably, it slipped through a crack in the floorboards, close to a distinctive-looking knot in the wood, and disappeared from view. Young Dr Clarence never saw it. He raged about the kitchen searching for it . . .

Back in the drawing room, Goose was startled by the abruptness with which Anthony let go of Dr Clarence's hand and tipped over backwards, his body going limp. Goose winced as Anthony hit a table. The table was heavy oak with chunky carved legs. It hardly moved as Anthony's dead weight bounced off it on his way to the floor. He convulsed for several moments, letting out what Goose thought sounded like a dying breath. Then, all of a sudden, Anthony became still.

Goose put his hands over his mouth as if to stop himself from screaming. He was genuinely concerned. 'Anthony,' he squeaked. He was quite sure he had just watched him die.

Dr Clarence moved fast. He jumped up and strode across to a cabinet, retrieving a dusty old medical bag from inside. He dashed back to Anthony, dropping to his side and dragging a stethoscope from the bag. As he reached out, Goose stopped him.

'Don't touch any skin!' Goose cried out.

Dr Clarence paused momentarily, nodded and then carefully positioned the diaphragm of his stethoscope on Anthony's motionless chest.

Frank and Goose looked at Dr Clarence, waiting for his diagnosis. It wasn't good. Dr Clarence was shaking his head and frowning. 'There's no heartbeat.' Goose let out an involuntary whimper.

'I'll call an ambulance,' said Frank, pulling out his mobile phone.

Goose looked on as Dr Clarence prepared to perform CPR. There was a swift determination to the doctor's movements. Rather than calming Goose, this worried him more. He could tell by Dr Clarence's body language that they didn't have much time. An ambulance wouldn't help. It wouldn't get here fast enough to save Anthony.

Goose wondered why he was so concerned. After all, he didn't really know this man, and not so long ago he was convinced he had stolen the thing Goose cared about most in the world. Maybe that was it, Goose told himself. He was only worried about Mutt. If Anthony died, how would he ever find Mutt? That made sense to Goose, but he wasn't entirely sure it was true.

Dr Clarence positioned the heels of his hands on

Anthony's chest and was just about to press down when Anthony suddenly dragged in a gasp of breath. Everyone froze.

Dr Clarence leaned back and waited. Frank stopped dialling. Goose grabbed a handful of Frank's sleeve. They all watched on tenterhooks. Then Anthony's eyes flickered open. The air of tension eased. Frank glowered at Goose's hands clutching at his coat and Goose let go, smoothing the leather.

Anthony held his head, clearly in a lot of pain. Gradually the pain seemed to subside. When Anthony eventually spoke, his voice was barely audible.

'You said you hadn't lost anything,' he croaked. Dr Clarence frowned and started shaking his head as if to say he hadn't. 'The kitchen. Under the floorboards.' Dr Clarence didn't know what Anthony could mean.

The door to the kitchen opened and Dr Clarence entered, followed by Goose. Anthony and Frank brought up the rear. Anthony pointed to a particular section of the floor where he had seen the envelope vanish. He saw the distinctive-looking knot marking the spot.

'There,' he said. 'With the knot that looks like Queen Victoria.'

'What? Queen Victoria?' said Dr Clarence. He followed Anthony's gaze and saw the knot. Truth be told, it had never occurred to him that it looked like Queen Victoria in profile. 'What's there?' asked Dr Clarence. 'I don't understand.'

Goose looked from Anthony to Dr Clarence and back again.

'She said she left you a letter.' Anthony's words sent a chill down Dr Clarence's spine. The doctor remembered the letter and the phone call perfectly. As if it was yesterday instead forty years ago. It's not easy to forget the worst day of one's life.

Goose looked on, not entirely sure he understood what was happening. A thousand thoughts raged through the doctor's mind and his confusion played out on his face. In the end, there was only one thing he wanted to know. Goose watched as he crossed to a drawer and took out a large flat-head screwdriver. He walked back and then, crouching down, he pushed the tip of the screwdriver through the crack in the floorboards and prised one up. Ancient nails protested as they were forced from their beds. Dr Clarence raised the board far enough to get his fingertips underneath and then wrenched the board free. He looked down into the cavity beneath. Anthony, Goose and Frank moved in and looked over his shoulder. They all saw the small envelope, yellowed with age, addressed to 'Rafe'. Dr Clarence let out a tiny, strangled cry. He reached down and picked up the letter.

Goose was shaking his head gently. *How did Anthony know that was there?* he wondered.

Frank helped Dr Clarence to his feet and he crossed to the table where he slumped down in the chair, turning the envelope over and over in his hand.

'You going to open it?' asked Goose, intrigued now to find out what was inside.

'She said she'd left it for me,' said Dr Clarence. 'I didn't believe her. I should have tried to find her.'

'Maybe you shouldn't open it,' said Anthony.

Dr Clarence looked up fiercely, but he saw, in Anthony's face, that the suggestion was borne out of compassion and nothing else. He relaxed and considered Anthony's words. He knew the man was probably right. No good would come from opening that letter. If his wife was telling him how much she despised him, then the hurt of forty years ago would come to life once again. If she was telling him that she loved him and wanted him to come to her, then the regrets of a wasted life would be almost too much to bear. But Dr Clarence knew he had no choice but to read the letter.

'There is a kind of system, believe it or not, Frank. Your book will be in the hallway by the mirror.'

Frank nodded. 'Thank you.' Frank, Goose and Anthony knew it was time to leave. They started to edge out of the room. Anthony was the last to go. Dr Clarence looked up at him.

'Who are you?' he asked.

140

Anthony shrugged. 'Wish I knew.' And, with that, Anthony left.

Frank and Goose were scanning the spines of all the books near the mirror in the hallway. There were a lot. Easily a thousand. Neither could see *The Happy Prince* anywhere. Anthony caught up to them and he joined in the search. He stood at a distance so he could see all the books before him and scanned back and forth, assessing them.

'They're chronological, and alphabetical by author,' he said.

'Your Dr Clarence has way too much time on his hands,' muttered Goose.

Frank smiled.

'That antiques programme said it was published seven years after the original, which was 1888,' said Anthony, studying the books. 'So that makes it 1895.' Anthony moved towards the end of the section, to the Ws. He plucked out Frank's book and handed it to him. 'There you go.'

Frank was brimming with gratitude. 'Mate, I just don't know what to say,' he said.

'You don't have to say anything,' said Anthony, and he headed to the front door.

Frank followed but Goose loitered, looking back through the open kitchen door, watching Dr Clarence as he opened the envelope and started reading the letter. Goose watched the old man dissolve into tears.

Goose followed Frank and Anthony outside. As he came down the steps, he was shaking his head. He looked at Anthony.

'I . . . He didn't . . . He didn't even know,' he said, stuttering to find the right words. 'How did you . . . ? You couldn't have known.' And in that moment, Goose believed. 'So if I give the bangle back, then I get Mutt back, right?'

Anthony shrugged. 'I don't know. Maybe.'

Goose considered these words. They made some sort of twisted sense in his head. 'Yeah.' He nodded. 'I give the bangle back, then I get Mutt back.' He was certain of it.

## 15

# FRANK SURPRISES EVERYONE BUT MOSTLY HIMSELF

'Did you know, in France, it's illegal to call a pig Napoleon,' said Anthony as he and Goose and Frank were walking. Frank and Goose turned to look at him. He hadn't doled out an interesting fact for a while now and it took them both by surprise. Also, it seemed to have very little relevance to anything they had been talking about. He wasn't finished there. 'And in Texas you can't graffiti on someone else's cow. I suppose that means it's okay to graffiti on your own cow, but don't take my word for it.'

'I'll be sure to check that before I graffiti on any cow

next time I'm in Texas,' said Frank with a smirk. He was walking on air. After living through the worst year of his life (the canal, losing his best friend, the breakdown, losing his job and Alice and Jemma, and now about to lose them permanently to the other side of the world) he was finally starting to feel that his luck was changing. After all, he had the book back. Everything would be fine now.

'Actually, you know what? I've always wanted to go to Texas. Well, you know, America generally. Never been. Maybe I'll book us a holiday.'

Anthony scratched behind his ear. 'I'm not sure I've got a passport. No idea where it could be if I do.'

'Not us, you muppet! *Us!* Me and Alice and Jem.'

'But they're off to Australia, aren't they?' asked Anthony innocently.

Frank chuckled and shook his head. He prodded Goose. 'He's not really paying attention, this one, is he?'

Goose chortled back, but wasn't altogether sure if he had missed something. 'But I thought they were going to Australia,' Goose said.

Frank stopped, which meant Goose and Anthony had to stop too. 'Bloody hell, you two. I've got this now, haven't I?' said Frank, pulling back one side of his coat to reveal *The Happy Prince* tucked securely into an inside pocket. Just the top of it was peeking out. 'Why d'you think I've been running around like a headless blue-arsed fly looking fer it? This gives me the upper hand.'

'What does that mean?' asked Goose.

'It means, I'll go see Alice in a few days and patch things up with her. Forty grand's a nice amount of money. We can start again. It'll be good for us.'

'So you're going to Australia too?' asked Goose, a little confused.

'No! No one's going to Australia. They're staying right here.'

'Okay,' said Goose, certain he had missed something crucial in this conversation. 'Why a few days? Why not now?'

'Well,' said Frank. 'Right now, it's just a book, innit? I know a bloke who knows a bloke who'll probably buy it. Cold hard cash, that's what'll make Alice sit up and take notice.'

'Hmmm,' said Anthony and Goose simultaneously, and instantly Frank felt less sure of himself. He was aware of it, mindful of the fact that it had taken very little to shake his confidence.

'What's that supposed to mean?' he asked.

Anthony shrugged. 'Doesn't mean anything.'

'Well, it means something. Definitely means something. Person doesn't go "Hmmm" just for the sake of it. And in bloody stereo too.' Frank was becoming increasingly defensive.

'Well . . .' said Goose, looking at Anthony, who gestured for him to carry on. 'If it was me and I had a chance to get my family back, I'm not sure I'd be mucking about.'

'Mucking about?' said Frank. 'I'm not mucking about. I just want to do it right.'

'Okay,' said Goose, shrugging.

Frank could see he was far from convinced. 'Look. I know what I'm doing, all right?' he said.

'If you say so,' said Goose.

'I do. I do say so. You're just a kid. I don't even know why I'm having this conversation.' With that, Frank stuffed his hands into his pockets and marched ahead. Goose and Anthony let him walk on for a dozen paces, watching him.

'It's not the right thing to do, is it?' asked Goose quietly.

'Maybe he's scared.'

'Scared?' Goose frowned. 'Scared of what?'

'Of the book not making any difference.'

'But it will. Course it will. It has to.'

'I don't know, Goose. We don't know what's gone on between Frank and his wife. Maybe it's gone too far to repair.' Anthony looked wistful for a moment. 'Come on.' Anthony gestured with a nod of his head and he started walking after Frank.

146

Goose let both of them walk on. He chewed at the inside of his cheek and tried to work out exactly what he thought of what Anthony had said. Could that be true? Was Frank clutching at straws? Desperately looking for the book because it gave him something to do? It was a horrible feeling to have no hope. He knew what that felt like. The difference was that there was absolutely no chance his family would ever come back on account of being dead. But Frank's . . . they were here . . . in Manchester . . . In fact, just a dozen or so streets away. If it was him, he'd go straight there. It made him think about the time he'd learned to ride his bike. He'd got a new bike for his sixth birthday: jet black with a flaming skull on a plastic shield attached to the handlebars, two wheels, no stabilizers. A proper bike. His first. Everyone had tried to teach him how to ride: his mum, his dad, Uncle Frank, even Jemma, who was the same age as him but had been riding a two-wheeler since she was four. Thing is, it didn't work. He couldn't do it. He was scared. More than scared. Terrified. All he could think about was all the things that could go wrong. If he fell over, he'd hurt himself. If he went too fast, he'd fall over and hurt himself. If he stopped too abruptly, he'd fall over and hurt himself. Take a corner too fast and he'd fall over and hurt himself. One by one they all gave up trying to teach him. He was a lost cause.

Then one day his dad took him to the park with the

147

bike. Maybe one last try. He didn't attempt to tell him what to do. He didn't hold on to the back and run along with him. Instead, he went and sat on a bench and read a book. He said to Goose: 'Look, thing is, you know *how* to ride a bike. You know how to make it go, you know how to make it stop and all the bits in between. Now the only thing stopping you from riding it is you. So I'm going to sit here and you go off and you teach yourself. All you have to do is get your head round it.'

With that, his dad had smiled and turned to his book. Goose had pushed the bike away, thinking about what his dad had said. At first, all his usual concerns were at the forefront of his mind, but then when he thought about it he realized his dad was right. All his friends could ride a bike, he thought. He would miss out on so much if he didn't do this. All he had to do was push off and get a fair amount of speed going. Without giving it too much more thought, he kicked the pedal round so it was at the right angle and stepped up on it, pushing down, bringing his other foot up on to the other pedal and pushing down on that one. Suddenly, he realized he was doing it. He was riding his bike. He rode about three times as far as he had planned to and came to a gentle, controlled stop. He lost his balance and tipped to the left but caught himself. He had done it.

He shunted the bike around in a tight circle and rode

back the way he had come. This time he cycled all the way to the end of the path where he had intended to stop, but he was enjoying himself and took the corner, not too fast, but steadily, and carried on. Twenty minutes later he rode past his dad.

'Awright, Dad?' he called as he went past. His dad smiled. Goose had done it. He had taught himself to ride his bike. All he had needed was someone to push him in the right direction. That's what his dad had done for him that day, Goose realized. He had given him an opportunity to do what he really wanted to do. In that instant, Goose knew what he had to do for Frank.

Frank was still marching ahead. Anthony was a short distance behind him, closer to Frank than he was to Goose. Goose slipped his hand into his pocket and pulled out his mobile. He went to his contacts and found Jemma. He dialled her number.

Across town, Jemma and Alice were in Sainsbury's doing some last-minute food shopping. Their trolley was half full. While Alice wandered off to grab some Brussels, Jemma's phone rang. She was surprised to see Goose's number come up.

'Hello, Goose. Everything all right?'

'Where are you?' asked Goose. 'You with your mum?'

'Err . . . yeah. We're in Sainsbury's. Why?' asked Jemma.

'How quick can you get home?'

'Well, Mum wants to go into town after this so we'll probably be a while.'

'No, that won't do. Can you get back in ten minutes?' asked Goose.

'What?' asked Jemma. 'I don't know. Why?' Then, as Jemma listened, Goose laid out all the relevant details of what was going on. A dozen different emotions played out over Jemma's face. She saw her mum coming back, carrying Brussels sprouts and a cauliflower.

'Mum's coming back,' she said into her phone. 'Gotta go.' She hung up quickly and shoved her phone back into her pocket.

'Who was that?' asked Alice as she placed the veggies into the trolley.

'No one,' said Jemma. 'Just Molly.'

Alice looked at her daughter and frowned. Jemma's face was pale. 'Are you okay, darling?' she asked.

Jemma shook her head. She spoke without being entirely sure what she was about to say. 'I think I'm going to be sick, Mum. Can we go home?'

'What? Sick how?'

'Please, Mum. Can we just go?'

'There's a toilet in here somewhere,' said Alice, putting a hand to Jemma's forehead and looking around.

'I don't want to go in a public toilet. Please, Mum. Can we just go home?'

Usually Alice wouldn't entertain such a preposterous request, but there was something about the look on her daughter's face that convinced her that she really did need to go home right away. Alice nodded. 'All right, come on.' With that, Alice pushed her trolley to one side and led Jemma out of the shop.

After hanging up his phone, Goose increased his pace so as to catch up with Anthony and Frank. Soon all three were walking together once again.

'Can I have a look at the book, Frank?' asked Goose.

'What?' Frank had been caught up in his own thoughts for the last several minutes, playing everything over in his head.

'Just quickly,' said Goose, trying to sound as casual as he could. 'I didn't really look at it before. I'll be really careful with it.' Frank opened his mouth to deny him, but Goose didn't give him the opportunity. 'After all, we did help you get it back.'

Frank's instinct was to say no and point out that Anthony was the one who helped him get it back. Goose hadn't really done a whole heap of anything, but that was unfair, he decided.

'Just a very quick look though, okay? I don't want to expose it to the elements too much.'

Goose nodded and watched as Frank reached into the

inner pocket of his leather coat and drew out the small, slim volume. He held it out to Goose, who took it very carefully, holding it just by the edges.

'Wow!' said Goose. 'Sure doesn't feel like it's worth so much.'

'Yeah, well, it is,' said Frank, eager to get it back in his pocket.

'Sorry, Frank,' said Goose.

'What d'you mean?' Frank had a puzzled look on his face. 'Sorry for what?'

'For this,' said Goose, and with that he spun on his heel and started running back the way they had come as fast as he could go.

'GOOSE!' Frank bellowed. 'NO! Come back with that!' He took off at speed, in pursuit.

Anthony was left alone. 'That was unexpected,' he said to himself aloud before hurrying after both of them.

Goose knew exactly where he was going. He took every short cut available, squeezing through gaps in fences where Frank couldn't follow so he would have to go the long way around. Goose made sure Frank was always able to keep him in sight but never got close enough for Frank to nab him. It didn't help Frank's pursuit that the forty cigarettes he smoked on average per day were making his lungs feel like shrivelled prunes that were wholly incapable of drawing anything resembling oxygen into them. After the first few blocks, Frank was wheezing too much to even shout after Goose.

Goose turned corner after corner, sprinting across busy roads and all the time keeping Frank a reasonable distance behind.

Frank couldn't believe what Goose was doing. Did he think this was a game? Why was Goose robbing him?

Goose turned into a road of well-kept terraced houses. He could see a red Peugeot 106 pulling up to the kerb at the far end of the street and he increased his speed.

Alice parked and looked over at Jemma, lolling listlessly in the seat next to her. Alice reached over and brushed the hair from Jemma's forehead. 'Come on, we're home, poppet.'

'What?' asked Jemma weakly, looking up. She spotted Goose running towards them and she knew their timing had to be just right. 'Just give me a moment, Mum.' And she lowered her head. Alice looked on with great concern.

Goose reached Alice's car and stopped. Frank was almost on top of him. Goose's sudden stop took him by surprise and he had to twist to avoid a collision.

'What the bloody hell are you playing at, Goose?' Frank barked.

Goose shrugged. 'Sorry, Frank. Don't know what came

over me.' And with that he handed him the book. It was at that precise moment that Frank's brain realized where they were. He turned to look at Alice's car at the exact same moment that Alice looked up. Their eyes met and she looked thunderous.

'What have you done?' said Frank softly to Goose.

With that, Alice was out of the car. 'What're you doing here, Frank? You know you're supposed to call before you come over. You agreed.'

Frank put up his hands in an attempt to mollify the oncoming storm that was his estranged wife.

'Now, Alice, I . . .' His mind was racing. What should he say? How should he play this? Bloody Anthony and his talk of cows, and pigs called Napoleon, and Goose snatching the book. Now Frank's head was a mess, while he had been so certain of himself just a dozen minutes ago.

'This isn't fair, Frank,' Alice was saying. 'Not to me, not to Jemma. You can't do this. It's intimidation.'

'It's not intimidation, it's—'

'What? What is it then?' asked Alice.

'I just . . .' *What?* His mind was blank.

The passenger door of Alice's car opened and Jemma stepped out. Frank smiled awkwardly and his voice softened. 'Hello, Jem, darling. You all right?'

'No, she's not actually,' snapped Alice. 'She's not feeling very well. I need to get her inside.'

Before Frank could express his concern or Alice could make a move, Jemma said, 'Actually I feel fine now.'

'What!?' asked her mother. 'You were dying ten minutes ago.'

'It passed,' said Jemma with a shrug.

Alice wheeled on Frank. 'Have you put her up to this?'

'No! I—'

'It was me.' Everyone turned to look at Goose, who had been trying to edge subtly towards Anthony, who was loitering a short distance away. 'I called Jem,' Goose said.

'This isn't anything to do with you, Goose. You shouldn't have done that,' said Alice, clearly still furious but holding back because she was talking to Goose and not Frank.

'Yes, I should,' said Goose defiantly. 'Someone had to. Frank's got something to say to you.'

All eyes turned to Frank. He glared at Goose, his jaw rigid.

'What is it, Frank?' asked Alice. Her tone had softened just a little, maybe in deference to Goose.

Frank considered the question. He heard Goose's words in his head and he looked down at the book in his hand. He looked up at Alice glaring at him, waiting for an answer, then back at the book. Then at Jemma, biting her lip. Then, finally, back at the book. ''Ere,' he said, holding it out to Alice.

Alice frowned as she looked at the proffered book but made no move to take it. 'Wow, thanks.' The sarcasm in her voice came across loud and clear.

'You don't understand,' said Frank. 'It's worth . . . a lot of money.' He nodded as if that would prove he was telling the truth. 'I saw it on the telly . . . forty grand . . . it's worth forty grand. Maybe more. One on the telly was a bit knackered.'

'You what?' Alice couldn't compute what he had said. Her natural instinct was to look for the angle Frank was playing. Was it some sort of sick joke? But she knew her husband well enough to know he wasn't lying right now.

'And it's for you,' Frank said again, moving the book closer to Alice. She took it this time, holding it as if it was made of snowflakes and in danger of vanishing from her grasp if she was too rough. 'For Australia.' Alice looked up sharply, staring into his eyes. She couldn't believe what she was hearing. Neither could anyone else. For Frank's part, he couldn't believe he'd just said what he had, but he already knew he didn't regret it. He wanted to do this. 'To help you and Jem make a new life for yourselves . . . or . . . whatever you want.'

Alice looked at Frank, then back down to the book, then back up at Frank. Her heart was beating a little too fast and she wasn't sure if it was excitement or something else.

'Are you okay?' she asked Frank. 'You're not really ill or anything, are you?'

'Nah, nothing like that,' said Frank, and then he smiled as he realized: 'Actually I feel great.'

Alice thought some more. 'Forty thousand? Are you sure? This isn't one of your – you know?' She meant flights of fancy. Like the time Frank decided he was going to breed chinchillas because some bloke at work had bought a couple as pets for his kids and paid fifty quid each. Turned out chinchillas make terrible pets. The bloke at work got rid of his after a month because they had spent most of the time living up the chimney; only venturing out at night to chew through the curtains, electrical cables and the sofa. By then it had been too late for Frank and he had bought ten of the little buggers.

'No,' said Frank. 'It's rare. Really rare.'

Jemma stepped forward and looked over her mother's shoulder. 'You used to read that to me. I remember.'

'Yeah,' said Frank, a happy smile spreading over his lips at the memory and the fact that Jemma still remembered. 'Mad, innit? It was worth all that money when we were struggling for every penny.'

'And you're just giving it to us?' asked Alice, who still couldn't believe it. 'To go to Australia?'

'Yeah,' said Frank with a nod. 'Happy Christmas.'

'But I thought you didn't want us to go,' said Alice.

'I don't,' said Frank. 'I'm going to miss you both like crazy, but if it's what you want then . . . that's what I want too. I just want you both to be happy.'

Jemma dashed forward and threw her arms around her father, hugging him tightly. Frank hugged her back and tears were starting to run down his face. Alice was trying hard not to start crying too. She reached out to touch her husband but pulled back at the last moment. The events of the last year made her cautious.

'Can Dad come in, Mum?' Jemma turned to her mother.

Alice hesitated just for a moment. Then she nodded. 'You want to come in?' she said to Frank. 'I'll put the kettle on, yeah?'

'Yeah, that'd be good,' said Frank. 'I'll be in in a minute.'

Alice nodded and she and Jemma headed inside, examining the book.

Frank turned to Goose and Anthony. 'I'm gonna nip in for a cuppa, like,' said Frank.

'Yeah, we heard,' said Goose. 'Can't believe you did that. What happened to having the upper hand and America and all that?'

'Don't know,' said Frank, grinning. 'It just seemed like the right thing to do. You want to come in as well?'

'I need to get the bangle, Frank,' said Goose.

Frank nodded. Then he reached into his pocket and

pulled out a roll of cash, which he stuffed into Goose's hand.

"Bout a hundred and fifty there. It's all I've got on me. I sold the bangle to Noel.'

'Noel?' Goose grimaced.

'I know. I know,' said Frank contritely. 'Don't let him do you. He only gave me forty.'

'Forty?' said Goose. 'But you gave me a hundred.'

Frank shrugged. 'Yeah, well, you know,' he said as casually as he could manage.

The bud of a thought flowered in Goose's head. *Yeah, well, you know?* No, he didn't know. Frank had paid him more than twice the bangle's value. Why would he do that? Goose knew the rest of the stuff wasn't worth a lot. Goose thought back to all the other things he had taken to Frank over the last year. That stamp collection that seemed pretty basic but Frank had assured him that there were some real rarities in there. He'd given him fifty pounds for that. Just at the right time too. It was near Nan's birthday and he was able to buy her that silk scarf she wanted. Then there was that vase he'd nicked from the semi-detached on Highdown Road. He was sure it was a piece of tat but Frank had given him eighty quid, which was lucky because Mutt had to go to the vet for his booster shots. And, in that moment, Goose put all the pieces together: Frank had been looking out for him all this time, giving him above and beyond. Goose had never seen it. Now he wondered how he could have missed it. Goose stared open-mouthed at Frank. All this time he had thought he was so alone, and now it turned out he never was. Goose threw himself at Frank, wrapped his arms around his waist and hugged him tightly. Frank put an avuncular hand on Goose's shoulder and smiled.

'Well, someone's gotta look after ya.'

Goose pulled away. If he hugged Frank any longer, he'd start crying. Everything Goose could think of to say at that moment seemed wildly inadequate so he didn't say anything at all. Frank understood perfectly. He looked at Anthony and smiled.

'And thanks. For everything. Thank you.'

'You're welcome,' said Anthony.

'Right, brew's waiting,' Frank said, and he turned and headed into his old home. He paused at the front door and looked back once. He smiled. Then he went inside. Anthony and Goose started to walk away.

'So who's this Noel then?' asked Anthony.

# 16

# TWO BEARS IN LEDERHOSEN DANCING ROUND A FISH

Helen pulled down a copy of Enid Blyton's *Five on a Treasure Island* from a shelf by the window of the small, cluttered bookshop.

'What about the Famous Five?' she said. 'I used love these when I was a girl.'

Milly poked her head out from behind a nearby display and shrugged. 'I don't know. What's it about?'

'It's about these children, Julian, Dick, Ann and George (George is a girl), and a dog called Timmy, who go on adventures. Usually to do with smugglers, far as I remember.'

'Maybe,' said Milly, and she disappeared from view again.

Helen retrieved her mobile from her handbag and glanced at the screen for the fifth time in less than two minutes. Still no message from Henry. How could he do this to her? Today of all days. Did he have no feelings left? She could feel the anger rising in her again as it had all day. She took a deep breath. She didn't want to be angry today. Not today.

Milly appeared at her side. 'What about that one?' she said, and pointed at a thin book with a garishly pink cover depicting a young ballerina. 'I like ballet dancers.'

Helen took the book from the shelf and studied the blurb on the back. She grimaced and flicked through the pages. 'I don't know. It's a little young for you. You were already more advanced than this.'

Helen felt eyes on her and turned to look at the young woman behind the counter. She had a stud above her lip, numerous earrings and the tip of a tattoo creeping up from beneath her collar. She was watching Helen out of the corner of her eye. Helen realized she had been talking aloud. She knew she did that when she was home alone, had caught herself a few times. She didn't realize she had started doing it in public.

The young woman with the stud called over to her: 'Can I help you find anything?' Her voice was nasal and disinterested. She didn't want to be stuck at work on Christmas Eve.

Helen shook her head, embarrassed. 'Just looking, thank you,' she said.

The young woman turned back to the gossip magazine in front of her but kept sneaking glances at Helen, concerned that she might be trouble.

Helen was wearing a red coat that came down to her knees, where it met the top of a pair of black leather boots. As always, she looked impeccable. She exuded poise and class so it was strange that she was now receiving suspicious looks from the pierced assistant.

Helen was carrying a large bunch of flowers. She shifted them from one arm to the other. She took her phone out one more time. Still nothing. Then she glanced out of the window and saw the number forty-seven bus pulling up.

'Oh, there's my bus,' she said as she headed to the door. The studded bookseller watched her leave, then glanced over to the shelf where Helen had been loitering to see if anything was missing. She quickly lost interest in that and returned to her magazine.

As Helen hurried out of the bookshop she collided with a broad man in a long army-style trench coat.

'I'm so sorry,' said Helen, not really looking at the

163

man, who was accompanied by a young boy. She ran on, reaching the doors of the bus just as they were closing. The driver opened them for her and she stepped on.

Anthony and Goose watched her go. 'Someone's in a hurry,' said Goose.

He had already forgotten all about the woman in the red coat as he turned to look up at a small antiques shop, nestled next to the bookshop. It looked a little too upmarket for the area. There was no gaudy sign, just a discreet brass plaque by the door. It read: 'Noel Noble – Purveyor of Rare Antiquities'.

'Prepare yerself,' said Goose out of the corner of his mouth. 'You're about to meet the slimiest man in Manchester.' Anthony looked intrigued as he read the brass plaque. 'Hmm,' Goose grunted. 'Purveyor of hooky crap, more like.'

Goose and Anthony entered the antiques shop. A small brass bell announced their presence.

'I'll be right with you,' called a rich, chestnutty voice from the back of the shop. Classical music was playing softly in the background. The shop was full of everything from jewellery to clocks to armoires, tables, urns, pots and chairs. The small space was overwhelmed by the sheer volume of stock. It looked cluttered.

Anthony glanced at Goose and saw him examining

the roll of money Frank had given him. Anthony gestured for Goose to put it away. Goose understood and did as instructed.

'Let's hope we've got enough,' he said quietly. 'Otherwise you'll have to dazzle him with some fact about ducks and . . . trousers.'

Anthony considered this. 'Don't know anything about ducks and trousers.' Then a thought occurred to him. 'Quackmore Duck is Donald Duck's dad, but he doesn't wear trousers.'

Goose couldn't help but smile.

They heard movement and turned to see Noel Noble approaching from the shadows and clutter at the back of the shop. 'I'm so sorry to keep you waiting. I was . . .' He stopped as he saw Goose and Anthony. His expression changed, as did his voice. Gone was the mellifluous tone, replaced with Noel's naturally harsh Glaswegian accent. 'What do yous want?' He was talking to Goose but looking at Anthony.

Noel was a small, thin man. His wavy hair was clearly dyed: a little purple around the edges and seriously thinning. He had arranged it in a sort of heavily lacquered pile on the top of his head. It fooled no one. He wore an expensive bespoke suit, but it was still too large for him. He was swamped by the material, which made him look all the more diminutive.

'I want to buy the bangle Frank sold you this morning,' said Goose.

Still looking at Anthony, Noel forced an uncomfortable laugh and returned to his unctuous purveyor-of-rare-antiquities lilt. 'Frank? I don't know any "Frank". Come on! Out with you.' And he tried to shoo Goose and Anthony towards the door.

Goose spun out of Noel's grasp. 'I said "buy", didn't I?' Anthony tried to speak up and tell Goose not to do what he was about to, but there was no chance. Goose plunged his hand into his pocket and pulled out the roll of cash. Noel's eyes lit up for an instant, but he was shrewd enough to hide his avarice.

'A bangle, you say.' Noel put a finger to his mouth and made a pantomime of furrowing his brow in deep thought. 'I don't seem to recall any bangles. I have a very nice broach. Early Victorian.' Noel was talking to Anthony. Goose realized this was because he didn't yet know who this stranger was and was trying to work it out before saying anything potentially incriminating.

'He's not the Old Bill, Noel. Look at him,' said Goose. Noel did look at Anthony and as soon as he stopped to think about it, he knew he wasn't a police officer. Still, no reason to abandon caution.

'Why would I care if he was the police? I have nothing to

hide.' Noel directed this last statement firmly in Anthony's direction.

'Come off it, Noel. You? Nothing to hide?' sneered Goose.

'Watch your tongue, boy.' And for a split second Noel's feral side was exposed. As a small man growing up in one of the rougher parts of Glasgow, Noel couldn't afford to be seen as weak. As a distinguished antiques dealer, he kept that side of his nature concealed, but it was there, bubbling just under the surface. Goose didn't yet understand that side of Noel.

'Awright, keep your hair on,' said Goose with a smirk. Anger flashed across Noel's eyes once more and he literally had to bite his tongue to keep his cool. 'Now we both know not everything in this place is a hundred per cent legal.'

'Nonsense!' spat Noel, doing his very best to appear insulted by the implied smudge on his character. 'I have receipts for everything.'

'Not everything,' said Goose. 'Not that clock over there, you don't.' He jabbed his chin in the direction of a large domed carriage clock. Below the clock face two gold-plated bears, dressed in lederhosen, danced round a fish that seemed to be leaping out of the sea. It was both ugly and ridiculous. 'I nicked that out of a house on Ashford Road for yer.'

'Get out!' barked Noel. 'Get out now!'

167

'Or that music box.' Goose turned his head, looking around the shop. 'Or that pocket watch. You want me to go on or shall I just make a whatchamacallit call to the police?'

'Anonymous,' said Anthony helpfully.

'Yeah, one of them,' said Goose.

'All right! All right!' said Noel, admitting defeat. There were just too many things in the shop that weren't entirely kosher for him to be able to clear them out in time if Goose did call the cops. 'I sold it.'

'You what?' Goose felt like crying. He had thought he was close to the end, close to getting Mutt back, but now he was moving further away. 'I don't believe you!'

'Believe me or not,' said Noel, shrugging, 'it's the truth. Of course . . .' Noel paused for maximum effect, the corners of his mouth flicking up in a reptilian smile, 'I might be able to recall who I sold it to . . .' One more pause. 'For the right price.'

Goose sighed. He was not surprised by this turn of events. Noel was only interested in money. It was always the bottom line with him. Goose took out the roll of cash, pulled off the rubber band holding it in place and peeled off two ten-pound notes and held them out. Noel shook his head.

'I don't remember for that much,' he said. Goose peeled off two more tenners and then two more. He held them out to Noel, who still shook his head. 'I remember for that much,' he said, indicating all of the money from the roll.

'That's a hundred and fifty quid!' said Goose. 'That's taking the—'

Noel cut him off. 'Take it or leave it.'

Goose knew he had no choice. He rolled the money up, reapplied the rubber band and handed the entire roll to Noel. 'There!' said Goose, barely able to rein in his anger. 'Now, who'd you sell it to?'

Noel tucked the money into a small pocket at the front of his waistcoat. He smiled, but only with his mouth. 'I sold it to . . . a woman carrying a bunch of red flowers.'

'That's it?' snapped Goose. 'For a hundred and fifty quid, that's all I get?'

'That's all I've got. She paid cash. You only just missed her. About ten minutes ago maybe.'

Goose looked as if he was about to hurl himself on to Noel and beat him senseless. Anthony intervened.

'It's all right. I know who she is,' he said.

Goose frowned at him. 'You know who she is? How do you know who she is?' he asked.

Noel didn't look happy. It wasn't so much of a victory if they knew who she was. As he was dealing with his disappointment, Anthony held out a gloved hand. His right.

'Mr Noble, thank you very much.' Instinctively Noel

169

went to take Anthony's offered hand. At the last second Anthony switched hands, offering his left instead. Without thinking, Noel switched hands too, but then Anthony switched back. Noel switched back. This odd little dance went on for several seconds longer. Goose looked on with curiosity. He thought of two people meeting in a doorway and both continuously trying to move out of the other's path but both repeatedly stepping in the same direction. Finally it came to an end and they shook awkwardly. 'Come on, Goose,' said Anthony. 'We'd better hurry.'

Goose and Anthony dashed out of the shop, leaving Noel all alone. He reached into the small pocket at the front of his waistcoat, but instead of the roll of cash he pulled out Anthony's smelly rolled-up sock. He dropped it quickly in disgust. He patted his other pockets, looking for the money. It took him several moments to realize it was gone.

Anthony and Goose strode quickly away from Noel's shop. Anthony opened his hand to Goose, revealing the roll of money. Goose couldn't believe it.

'Wicked!' he said. 'Is that what all that hand-shaking was about? Where'd you learn to do that?'

Anthony shrugged. He didn't have an answer. 'Don't know. Must've picked it up somewhere.'

'Like all the fascinating facts?'

'Yeah, I guess so.' Anthony stopped at the kerb and looked back along the road. The traffic was heavy.

'So who's the woman with the flowers?' asked Goose.

'No idea.'

'What?' Goose couldn't believe it. 'But you said—'

'Well, I don't know her name, but we saw her. She was the one who bumped into me. Red coat. Big bunch of flowers.'

Goose thought back to earlier and remembered the incident, but he hadn't paid the woman much attention at the time so couldn't recall very much about her. 'How does that help? She could be anywhere by now.'

'She got on a bus. Number forty-seven.'

'Right.' Goose still didn't see how they were going to find her.

'Ah, here it is,' said Anthony. Goose followed his gaze and saw another number forty-seven bus approaching. 'I say we get on and see where the route takes us.'

Goose wasn't sure, but as he looked behind him he saw Noel coming out of his shop with a face the same shade as an aubergine. It seemed like a good time to leave.

Goose and Anthony sat on the top deck of the bus, at the front, each with their own seat, one either side of the aisle. They watched the world outside go by as the sun was beginning to set.

'It's Christmas; she could have been going anywhere,' said Goose, feeling very much like his glass was not so much half empty as someone had come along and thrown his glass on to the floor, smashed it and danced about in its remains singing, 'Na-na-na-na-na!'

'People don't go just anywhere with flowers,' said Anthony, pushing the positivity in his voice in an attempt to combat Goose's negativity. It didn't work.

'At Christmas they do,' said Goose sullenly.

'Maybe we'll get lucky,' said Anthony.

'And maybe we won't,' said Goose. 'This goes every-where.' He meant the bus.

'Then we'll go everywhere with it,' said Anthony.

Goose slumped back in his seat and huffed. Then he leaned forward, wiped the condensation from the window in front of him with his sleeve and slumped back into position once more, also huffing again for good measure.

They travelled like that in silence for several minutes. Gradually Goose's icy mood started to thaw and soon he forgot he had the hump. A question had been flitting about his head for a while now. He looked at Anthony out of the corner of his eye, wondering whether or not he should ask it. In the end, he decided he should.

'Can I ask a question?' said Goose.

'Well, you just did, so clearly the answer is yes, you can.'

'Right.' Goose wasn't sure if Anthony was making fun of him or if he was now cross.

'Is there another one?' said Anthony. 'Question, I mean.' He smiled and didn't look cross.

Goose felt it was okay to carry on. 'Yeah, well . . . it's just . . . What's it like when you have a . . . you know . . . vision thingy?' he asked. 'I mean, it doesn't last very long, but you seem to see a whole bunch of stuff.'

'How long does it last?' asked Anthony.

'A couple of seconds maybe,' said Goose. 'You go . . .' And he mimicked the sharp intake of breath he had heard Anthony do three times now. 'Then your eyes sort of roll back and you fall over. And that's it.'

'Hmm,' said Anthony. 'Seems a lot longer to me.'

'So what's it like?'

'Well, it starts with this feeling that I'm suddenly moving really quickly. Kind of like I'm on a roller coaster and it's just gone *sssscccchhhhhhooooo.*' Anthony made a hand gesture to complement the sound effect, like the car of a roller coaster cresting over a hill and letting gravity do its thing. 'I feel all sort of weightless. Then there's the pain. It feels like something growing inside me or burrowing through me.' Goose scowled as he imagined what that was like. 'And then I get to where I'm going, the pain stops and it's sort of like a dream. I'm there but no one can see me. I can be standing right in front of them and they look right

173

through me. But it's not my dream. It's theirs. It's like I've snuck in and I'm watching their memories.'

'That sounds freaky,' said Goose.

'It is.'

They carried on for a little longer. Then it was Anthony's turn to ask a question.

'Tell me about Frank,' said Anthony. 'How do you know him?'

'He's my uncle,' said Goose. 'Well, not really. He's just always been Uncle Frank. He was my dad's best friend. They grew up together down south. Don't usually tell people my dad was a Southie. Or that he supported Chelsea.

'Parents can be embarrassing.'

'Tell me about it.' Goose almost gave into a smile, but thought better of it and pushed it away. He went back to talking about Frank. 'Dad and Uncle Frank knew each other their whole lives. Dad was the sensible one. That's what everyone said. Frank was a bit wild when he was younger. Always getting into bother. Dad was always sorting him out. Looking out for him.' Goose stopped and thought about how Frank was doing the same for him now. Uncle Frank had been one of the most important people in his dad's life. He had loved him like a brother. No, more than a brother. 'You can't choose family,' his dad had often said. Goose was starting to understand what he meant by that now. 'Dad got him a job. They were both firemen till . . .' Goose gnawed at the skin to the left of his finger-nails. 'Till the accident.'

'Why'd Frank give up?' asked Anthony.

'Something happened. Something that shouldn't.' He stopped speaking and Anthony wondered if that was all he was going to say. Then Goose said something else. 'Something bad.' He turned away and looked out of the window beside him. Anthony knew that conversation was over.

Suddenly Goose sat up straight and rubbed at the window to clear it. He looked out at a massive cemetery that stretched to the horizon on both sides of the road.

'Flowers,' said Goose.

## 17

# WALT DISNEY WAS AFRAID OF MICE

The cemetery gates were made from wrought iron bent into the shape of a choir of angels; some were playing horns, one even had a harp. The gates were large enough to allow a hearse and other funeral cars to pass through. There was a smaller pedestrian doorway within the main gates, but to go through that you had to open and step through an angel and in doing so separate its body from its head, which was a little disconcerting.

Anthony stepped through and gazed around. The cemetery was huge. There was a small chapel a little way off to his left. It was surrounded with scaffolding and two burly builders were at the top, working on the roof.

A third builder was on the ground, stoking a bonfire where he seemed to be burning old roof joists. The tinny sounds of Radio One blared from a radio tied on to the scaffolding, disturbing what was otherwise an oasis of whiteness and silence. An undisturbed blanket of snow spread out before him. Bare trees stood out, crooked and grey.

'So which way?' said Anthony. When he didn't get a response he turned to see what had become of Goose. He saw he was still outside the gates. He looked younger than Anthony had ever seen him look. He looked like a little boy, pale and scared. 'What's wrong?'

'My mum and dad are here,' said Goose in a whisper.

Anthony strolled back. He stood alongside Goose for several moments without saying anything. Then: 'Did you know Walt Disney was afraid of mice?'

Goose's brow wrinkled as he considered that statement. 'What does that mean?' he asked.

'And Thomas Edison was afraid of the dark.'

Goose put his hands out and shrugged, unable to find another way of saying, 'What are you going on about?'

'He was afraid of the dark so he invented the light bulb. Walt Disney was afraid of mice and he created the most famous mouse in the world.'

'So?' asked Goose, wondering if this was leading somewhere.

'So,' said Anthony, 'sometimes you have to run towards the things that make you want to run away.'

Finally Goose understood what Anthony was trying to say. He took a deep breath and nodded.

'Come on then,' he said, and strode through the open angel gate. Anthony followed.

They left the chapel behind and walked on. The hustle and bustle of the busy city soon became a distant memory. A cocoon of muffled sounds surrounded them. The only noise came from clumps of snow toppling from the thin branches of the naked trees and the occasional bird chirruping as it sought out hard-to-come-by food.

As they reached the apex of a small hill and looked down into a wide, shallow valley below they saw hundreds of graves stretching out before them. The ground here was uneven and the gravestones were spaced randomly. They looked like raggedy black teeth in a vast white mouth. Dozens of skeletal trees stood hauntingly, waiting for spring to dress them again.

Goose nudged Anthony and pointed with his chin. Helen was easy to pick out in her red coat. She stood out against the white and black. She was crouching by a grave, arranging the flowers she had bought. Even from this distance Goose and Anthony could tell she was sobbing. She stood up and wrapped her arms around herself. She glanced back towards Anthony and Goose but paid them no attention. Clearly they were not who she was looking for and appeared to Helen like just another couple of mourners coming to visit their lost ones on Christmas Eve.

Helen ran a hand through her hair and wiped her eyes. She blew a kiss towards the gravestone and then turned and walked off.

Anthony and Goose waited for several moments and then followed. As they passed the grave where Helen had been Goose stopped and read the inscription:

EMILIA IRIS TAYLOR
'MILLY'
BELOVED DAUGHTER OF HELEN
AND HENRY TAYLOR
BORN 16TH JUNE 2004
DIED 24TH DECEMBER 2010

A shiver ran down Goose's spine and a cloud of cold breath burst from his mouth like a milky bubble. Anthony wasn't blind to Goose's reaction. He read the stone.

'She died the same day as your parents,' he said. Goose nodded weakly, but that wasn't what had startled him. He knew who Milly Taylor was, but he didn't say anything to Anthony.

Goose looked up and saw the tip of Helen's head disappearing over the hill.

'Come on,' he said to Anthony, and they hurried after her.

Anthony and Goose watched as Helen entered the chapel. One of the builders gestured to his friend, nodding towards the radio. He switched it off respectfully.

The chapel was small. Just one room, about seven metres by five, but the ceiling was high. There were tall, narrow stained-glass windows, four on either side. The late sun shone through them from the west, casting exquisite patterns across the dozen or so pews.

Helen walked slowly up the aisle, turning at the head of the pews to a banked side altar where dozens of votive candles were displayed around a large statue of the Blessed Virgin. She took a taper from a thin fluted glass, lit it on an already burning candle and ignited the dormant wick of another. She extinguished and then discarded the taper in a bucket of sand beneath the altar. She bowed her head and prayed silently.

As she was praying, she was not aware of Anthony and Goose entering the chapel. They closed the door behind them, standing quietly in the entrance, watching her. Goose looked uncomfortably at Anthony.

'What now?' he whispered. 'We can't just go and ask her for the bangle. She'll think we're nutters.'

Anthony stared at Helen, turning an idea over and

over again in his mind. He knew what he had to do, but it was like someone suggesting he thrust his hand into a nest of angry snakes. It wasn't going to be pleasant.

'Stay here,' he said to Goose. He was scared and the words came out riding on the tip of his breath. Goose watched as Anthony started to remove the glove from his right hand. Goose grabbed his sleeve and pulled him back, shaking his head.

'You can't,' he said, genuinely concerned for Anthony's well-being. 'You didn't see yourself at Dr Clarence's. They're getting worse. I'm not sure you'll wake up from another one.'

Anthony smiled, touched by Goose's concern. 'Trust me,' he said. 'I think I'm getting the hang of it now.'

Goose let go of Anthony's sleeve and watched with worry etched deep into his face as his strange friend moved quietly up the outer aisle, to the left of the pews, making his way softly to the side altar.

A tear slid down Helen's cheek and dripped from the curve of her top lip, falling to the stone floor. It flattened, dark against the masonry, as she finished her prayers for her daughter. She wiped her eyes as she raised her head and turned away. She gasped as she saw Anthony close behind her. She stumbled, her hand reached out instinctively to steady herself and Anthony caught it. He drew in a sharp breath and his eyes grew wide. It felt as if molten metal was flooding into him through his fingers, filling him up, expanding as it solidified, pushing out his bones, muscles and flesh until he felt his skin was about to tear open. In his mind, he screamed.

# 18

# ON THIN ICE

Anthony opened his eyes and he was lying face down on a lawn. The grass was sharp with frost and his teeth chattered as the cold threaded through him. As he changed his focus and his field of vision expanded, he saw a pair of strange pink creatures mottled with purple spots. Their eyes followed him. He lifted his head from the frozen ground and now saw that they were a pair of monster slippers. He tilted his head up and saw that they belonged to a pretty little girl about six years old, with a head of curls and bright blue eyes. She was wearing a voluptuous, fluffy dressing gown, also pink, and the chill didn't seem to affect her. She didn't look down at Anthony. She couldn't see him. He was a ghost to her. He knew somehow that this was Milly Taylor and this was the day she died.

Milly took a tentative step forward and the grass crunched beneath her large colourful slippers. Anthony raised himself up on to all fours and looked down the length of the garden. At the end, he saw what had attracted Milly's attention: a door in the high fence stood ajar, creaking softly back and forth, calling out to her.

'Don't go,' said Anthony, but of course she couldn't hear him. She sped up, running now. Anthony followed.

Milly emerged from the door in the high fence and looked out with a sense of wonder. The Taylors' house stood by a canal. There was no one around, and as Milly tiptoed forward she came to the edge of the canal and looked down. It was frozen solid. Milly looked in both directions. The canal was white and looked like something out of a fairy tale.

The low early-morning sun shone down and glinted on something metal embedded in the frozen water. The glinting caught Milly's eye and she squinted to try to make out what it was. Anthony came and stood next to her as she looked around and saw a smooth brown stone about the size of an egg nestled in the overgrown border of the path running alongside the canal. She picked it up and held it out over the edge, letting it drop. It landed with a deep, reverberating thud. It sounded to her like the canal was firm.

Anthony shook his head. He didn't want to see this. There was nothing he could do to stop what was about to happen. He wasn't really there. He knew that.

'Don't go down there,' he said, even though he knew it was futile. Milly trotted past him to a rusty old ladder fixed to the wall of the canal, disappearing beneath the water level. Anthony stood at the top of it, impotent, as Milly turned round and stepped back on to the first rung. The old ladder shifted a little under her weight. The brackets holding it to the wall were worn. One of these days it would just come away. It rained rusty dandruff down on to the ice. She lowered her foot to the second rung and brought her other foot to meet it. The ladder groaned some more but it didn't buckle.

Anthony couldn't stay still. He knew Milly was about to die, but he didn't know how or when exactly. Every next step could be her last. Watching her was torturous.

The little girl climbed slowly but confidently down the nine rungs until finally she was able to place a tentative fluffy pink toe on to the frozen water. She applied pressure little by little, still keeping a firm grip on the rails of the ladder just in case. Her second foot came down and joined the first. Now she was standing on the ice.

'One. Two. Three,' she counted under her breath, and then she let go of the ladder. Nothing happened. She hopped once, landing as lightly as she could. Everything felt secure beneath her so she jumped again, more vigorously this time. The ice felt thick.

Anthony watched from above as Milly turned and looked out across the frozen canal. She saw the glinting metal again. It was only about two metres away from her, but because the sun was shining on it she still couldn't work out what it was. She took a half-step forward. Planting her foot, heel to toe, slowly, still testing the validity of the ice. Then another step. And another. The canal continued to feel safe.

At about the halfway point between the ladder and the glinting object the ice started to thin. Unfortunately, because of her hefty slippers, Milly couldn't feel the cracks that were starting to spread out beneath her weight. A spider's web of fissures extended underneath every footfall. The tiny cracks moved quickly and met up with their neighbours, at which point the cracks would double in size.

Anthony looked away. He brought his hands up to his face, desperate to shield himself from seeing what was about to happen.

Milly took another step forward and she was standing over the metal treasure. She reached down and discovered it was just a bottle top. She wrenched it out of the ice and looked at it, frowning with disappointment. She tossed it away and turned to head back to the ladder. As she took her first step, there was an almighty crack, like the sound of

186

a bullwhip. The noise echoed through her and around her. Milly screamed and stood perfectly still.

She looked down and could see how thin the ice now was beneath her feet. It was just millimetres deep and there was fluid water below. Like an army of small, scurrying insects the cracks spread out rapidly, emanating from her. Milly was paralysed with fear . . .

Anthony found himself standing at the foot of Henry and Helen's bed just as Helen Taylor woke with a start, as if from a bad dream. She couldn't remember any of it if it was a dream, but she was left feeling anxious so she knew it must have been a bad one.

'Milly's in trouble. You have to get up,' said Anthony breathlessly, but of course Helen couldn't hear him.

Helen looked at Henry snoring softly next to her and then pulled back the heavy duvet and swung her legs out. She reached down and grabbed her fat, cushioned slipper boots and pulled them on.

She padded along the hallway with Anthony following her and stopped at Milly's room. The door was wide open and Helen poked her head in. She was surprised to discover that Milly's bed was empty.

'She's not there,' said Anthony. 'She's gone downstairs. Outside. On the canal.'

Helen stepped back out on to the landing and moved

towards a frosted glass door at the end of the corridor. She pushed the door open and looked into the white-and-green tiled bathroom. It was empty too.

'No!' Anthony howled with frustration.

Helen stopped and listened to the sounds of the house. It was silent. It was as if Milly didn't exist. A shiver ran down Helen's spine.

'Mills?' she called, but there was no answer. She headed downstairs, hastening her gait a little as she went . . .

Helen reached the expansive entrance hall at the bottom of the stairs. Anthony was already there, standing next to a towering Christmas tree.

'Milly?' called Helen, sticking her head into the empty lounge, hoping to see Milly sprawled on the sofa reading a book or on the floor playing with her dolls. But the room was empty.

'Go to the kitchen,' Anthony pleaded.

Helen stepped back into the hallway and looked along to the kitchen at the end. She felt a draught snaking around her ankles.

'Milly?' she said quietly and moved swiftly towards the kitchen . . .

Finding the back door open, Helen stepped out into the garden. Anthony was there already. The first thing Helen saw was the trail of Milly's footprints leading down the frosty grass. She looked and saw the gate at the end of the garden swinging back and forth in the early-morning breeze.

'Oh God! MILLY?' she called as she ran down the garden. 'HENRY!' She turned and screamed back at the top of her lungs. Anthony watched her go. Even though he knew this had already happened and couldn't be changed, he still hoped for a miracle . . .

A Mercedes fire-rescue truck skidded to a stop on the towpath and two firemen scrambled out. Anthony walked amongst the gathered neighbours and general rubberneckers who had come to watch the drama unfold. He immediately recognized the first fireman. It was Frank. He looked more robust than Anthony was used to seeing him. His hair was tidier and his skin looked healthier. It wasn't yet addled by alcohol.

'Hello, Frank,' said Anthony, even though he knew Frank couldn't hear him.

Frank reached the edge of the canal and stopped next to Helen at the top of the ladder. He looked down and saw Henry in his dressing gown and slippered feet down on the ice, holding on to the ladder with one hand and reaching out to tiny, terrified Milly with the other. Milly hadn't moved. She stood statue-like in the middle of the frozen water surrounded by a rapidly expanding web of cracks

189

and fissures. Every little movement Milly made caused the ice to splinter more. She was so scared but held back the tears for fear that the motion of sobbing would rupture the ice still further.

A wave of relief washed over Helen as she saw Frank and his partner approaching. 'Oh thank God,' she said, grasping Frank by the arm and holding the material of his sleeve tightly. 'Please help her!'

Frank smiled reassuringly. 'Don't worry, it'll all be fine.' Frank turned and looked down the ladder at Henry. 'Come back up, please, sir. I can handle this.' The confidence in Frank's voice buoyed Henry and he nodded up to Frank. He turned to Milly.

'It's okay now, poppet. This nice fireman's come to help you.'

'Daddy, don't go!' whimpered Milly, still not moving.

'It's fine,' said Henry, his voice choking a little. 'It'll all be fine.'

'Come on, please, sir,' called Frank. Time was of the essence. He didn't know how much longer that ice would hold. It was a miracle that it'd held together this long. Henry nodded to Milly and then turned and climbed the ladder. Milly let out a little whine and followed with her eyes only as her father reached the top of the ladder and was helped up by Frank. She saw Frank stripping off all unnecessary clothing. He discarded his helmet, jacket and

190

boots in order to make himself as light as possible. Then he climbed on to the ladder. His partner came up behind him and attached a steel cable from the truck to the back of his belt. Frank descended facing forward, looking at Milly and the frozen canal.

'It's all right, miss,' he said, forcing a lightness into his voice. 'My name's Frank. What's your name?'

Frank reached the bottom of the ladder and placed a foot on the ice. The freezing cold instantly penetrated his sock and stung his sole. He ignored the sensation and brought his other foot down. The ice felt solid beneath him.

'What's your name?' Frank asked again.

'M-Milly,' she stuttered.

'That's a nice name, said Frank casually. Not a hint of anxiety in his tone. He let go of the ladder and moved forward tentatively, testing the ice with each step. 'How old are you, Milly? Five? Six?'

'Six,' breathed Milly.

'Six. You got a job yet?'

The question surprised Milly and for a moment she forgot where she was and laughed. 'No,' she said.

'Married?' asked Frank. Milly actually smiled and shook her head. The shake was just a little too vigorous and the ice growled. Frank froze. Milly cried out. Helen turned her head into Henry's shoulder and closed her eyes. The moment passed and the ice didn't break.

'I've got a little girl. Bit older than you. My Jemma's ten.' Frank edged forward slowly. The soles of his feet were burning, but he ignored the pain. He reached out his hand. He was only inches away now. 'Take my hand,' said Frank. 'Come on. Reach out.' Frank continued to move forward. Just another few seconds and he would have her.

Then, with a roar, the ice exploded.

Helen and Henry screamed as Milly and Frank vanished from sight. The onlookers gasped. Anthony hung his head.

Beneath the surface of the canal, the subzero temperature was a huge shock to Frank's system. His chest contracted, pushing all the air out of his lungs. In a second, he was disorientated. He couldn't tell which way was up. Then he saw Milly. Her dressing gown had come open and her nightdress was ballooning around her. She was screaming in terror and panicked air bubbles poured out of her mouth. Frank reached out to her as she sank into the gloom at the bottom of the canal. His fingertips brushed through her hair and then suddenly Frank was snatched backwards, away from her. He saw Milly one last time as she was consumed by the darkness below.

One of Milly's monster slippers broke the surface first and floated there. A moment later Frank emerged as the cable from the fire-rescue truck hauled him up. He coughed and spluttered, vomiting freezing canal water.

Helen and Henry stood immobile, waiting to see if he had their daughter. When they saw he was empty-handed, Helen screamed and started to wail with anguish. Henry dropped to his knees and started to sob. Helen ripped off her dressing gown and ran to the edge of the canal. Henry tried to stop her, but he wasn't fast enough. She jumped in, arcing over Frank's head. He tried to make a grab for her but his movements were slow because he was so cold. The ice splintered beneath her as she entered the water.

The freezing temperature was worse than Helen could ever have expected. As she sank lower the light from above faded. She couldn't see further than an arm's length in front of her, and the deeper she went the darker it became.

Up above, Henry was teetering on the edge of the canal. He wanted to go in after his wife and daughter, but he couldn't. Fear was holding him back.

'Bri!' Frank called up to his partner through chattering teeth. 'Give me some slack.' Frank's partner reversed the winch and the cable connected to Frank's belt loosened. Fists tightly clenched, his whole body shuddering, Frank made his way to the hole in the ice where Helen had gone through. He took a series of short breaths, then the largest breath he could manage and he let himself topple head first back into the icy water.

Under the water, Helen was panicking. There was barely any air left in her lungs, but she didn't even notice.

She was panicking because there was no sign of Milly. It was so dark down here that Milly could have been right next to her and she wouldn't see her. She reached out with her hands, scrabbling desperately for something of her daughter. Unconsciousness was enveloping her like a cloud. Soon she would be helpless. Her eyes started to close and her mouth started to open. Ice water was beginning to flood her lungs. Helen was about to die. She wasn't aware of Frank's hand as it found the cotton of her nightdress and gripped it tightly. Helen started to rise up.

Frank broke the surface and roared with the pain of the cold. His partner, Brian, was on the ice to help him get Helen up and out of the water. Henry was there too, having bridled his fear. Brian thrust a thermal blanket into his hands and instructed him to wrap his wife in it, which he did while Brian pulled Frank out of the water. He wrapped him in a thermal blanket as well, but Frank pushed him away. He was shivering violently.

'Her,' was all he could manage to say, gesturing towards Helen. Brian understood. He hurried over to Helen and started to perform CPR. Frank looked on, wrapping himself more tightly in the blanket. He caught Henry looking at the hole in the ice and the darkness below. He was looking for his daughter. He turned and caught Frank's gaze.

'I'm sorry,' said Frank, and he closed his eyes, choking back the tears . . .

194

# 19

# THE ANGEL AT THE ALTAR

Anthony's eyes rolled back into his head so only the whites were showing and he pitched backwards, landing hard, spreadeagled on the altar. Every muscle in his body was convulsing as if he was in the grip of an epileptic seizure. Helen looked on in horror. To her this had all happened in less than a second. She had turned, this strange-looking man was standing behind her, he had steadied her as she stumbled and then he had collapsed.

She sensed movement from the corner of her eye and twisted her head just as Goose appeared. He dropped to Anthony's side.

'Anthony? Can you hear me?' he said. 'Anthony?'

'Is this your father?' asked Helen. Goose looked

up at her and shook his head. 'What's wrong with him?'

'He should be okay in a minute,' said Goose, quietly praying to a God he had long ago stopped believing in.

Gradually Anthony's spasms lessened until it seemed he was just asleep. His breathing took a little longer to even out. His lips parted and riding on the tip of a breath he uttered a single word: 'Milly'.

Helen felt a chill pass right through her. 'What did he say?' she asked, but she knew exactly what he had said. 'What do you . . . ?' She paused, running everything through in her head. Something wasn't right. She felt a sudden surge of anger blister inside her. 'Who are you two? Where have I seen you?' In her mind she whirled back through the day. She didn't have to go very far. She remembered where she had seen them: back in the cemetery, but before that outside the bookshop. She had bumped into Anthony as she ran for the bus. 'Is this some sort of sick joke?'

Goose looked up at her again. He didn't know what to do. His concern for Anthony was distracting.

'The bangle,' said Goose, and Helen stepped back and put a protective hand on her bag. 'It wasn't Noel's to sell.'

'How do you know about the bangle?' asked Helen. Her mind raced to put the pieces together. There was only one explanation that made sense. 'You've been following me.'

'Yes, but—'

Helen scrambled through her bag and pulled out her mobile phone. Goose stood up and Helen took a nervous step backwards.

'You stay where you are,' she said, holding up a finger. 'I'm calling the police.'

'Please don't,' said Goose. 'It's not what you think.' Goose couldn't find the right words to explain himself. 'I know who you are. When I saw the grave. Milly's grave.' An involuntary shudder ran through Helen as Goose said her daughter's name. 'It's all my fault, you see. It was my fault she died.'

Strong words. Helen's head was a mess. She let the hand holding the phone drop to her side.

'What are you talking about?' she said quietly.

'It should have been my dad who came to you that day. He would have saved her. My dad could have saved anyone. But I hid his keys, you see.'

Helen didn't know what Goose was talking about, but there was something about him that made her believe he was telling the truth.

Just then, Anthony groaned as he started to regain consciousness. Goose looked down at him, then turned back to Helen.

'He's bringing everything together again.' Goose paused to wipe his nose on his sleeve. 'So he can make it right. He is. If I hadn't hidden the keys, my dad would have driven himself, and he would've gone some other way or something else would have happened and he and Mum wouldn't have died. I didn't mean for them to die. I didn't mean for anyone to die.' He looked soulfully at Helen.

The anger within her evaporated as she saw Goose's pain. She reached out to him.

'It's all right,' she said. 'It wasn't your fault.'

'It was,' said Goose in an almost inaudible voice.

Helen shook her head. 'No. *No*. I should know. I forgot to lock the gate, you see. We always locked the gate. Accidents happen.' She didn't really believe what she'd said. Not as far as she was concerned, at least. Her mind drifted to her room of recrimination: a place she went to often. It was a cold and inhospitable place. A place where she could punish herself. *WHY hadn't she heard her daughter getting up? WHY hadn't she heard her going down the stairs and outside? WHY did they live in such a big house where she couldn't hear the back door being unlocked? WHY had she left the key in the door? WHY hadn't she padlocked the back gate? Why? WHY?* **WHY?** For a year now, these questions and a hundred more just like them would torment her morning, noon and night. Sometimes she couldn't sleep because the questions were being asked so loudly and aggressively.

She would try to dull the questions with wine, but that didn't always work. The buzz from the alcohol would wear off in the early hours and she would be awake at four in the morning with her husband snoring next to her and those incessant questions for company. And four in the morning was the loneliest time of all. That was when she would dig her fingernails into the flesh of her forearm and tear at her skin until she bled. The pain was fleeting, but it was the only thing that took her mind elsewhere. She hadn't worn short sleeves all year. Henry hadn't noticed.

Helen realized she had drifted into her thoughts when she caught Goose staring at her.

'The bangle,' he said, struggling to find the right words. 'I-it wasn't Noel's to sell. It was . . .' The word stuck in his throat, but he knew he had to say it. 'Stolen.'

He saw Helen react to that the way honest people should react to discovering something they have is stolen. He saw a mixture of alarm, disgust and confusion play across her face. Goose knew there was no way he could get through this without telling her the whole story, but he so didn't want to. There was something about Helen that reminded him of his mum. Not the way she looked or sounded, but there was a warmth to her that made him feel safe. He wished he could give in to that, let her envelop him in her arms, stroke his hair and tell him everything was going to be okay. That's what his mum used to do when he had a bad dream. Sometimes he used to pretend that he'd had a nightmare and cry out in the night so she'd come running. He didn't do it often. Just once or twice when he was awake in the night and needed that feeling of security, his mother's reassurance.

But he knew that wasn't going to happen. He had to finish what he'd started. He had to tell Helen the rest. He felt confident that she wouldn't scold him when he told her. He was more afraid of seeing a look of disappointment in her expressive eyes.

Goose took a deep breath and summoned the strength to say just six little words, but they were the hardest six words he could remember having to say for a long time.

'It was me who stole it.'

Goose looked down at his feet after that, studying the weave of his laces. Considering the aglets. That actually made him smile, but not strongly enough to show on the outside.

'Oh,' said Helen. The suspense was torturous. Goose had to look at her to see if she hated him now. His neck muscles didn't seem to want to comply as he slowly raised his head. He looked at her. He didn't see reproach in her face. He wasn't sure what he saw. It might have been understanding, maybe even acceptance. Goose wanted to touch her. He wanted her hand to surround his protectively.

200

His hand started to jerk forward but it only moved a fraction before he stopped and brought it back. It was too much to expect.

'I have to give it back, you see. Belongs to an old lady and it's very special to her. I shouldn't have taken it. I know it was wrong, and I have to make it right.'

He considered what he had said and he was happy with it. He had said everything he needed to and had said it well enough. Then an afterthought occurred to him and he dug into his pocket. 'Here! I have money. I'll buy it off ya.'

'She doesn't want money, Goose.' Anthony's tired voice came from behind him and startled both of them. They turned to see that he was standing now. Neither had noticed him getting up. He was silhouetted against the dying light coming through the windows and, in his long coat, he had something of the air of an angel about him. 'She bought it for Milly,' Anthony said as he stepped forward into the light. Helen felt a surge of adrenalin flow through her at the sight of him. He made her heart beat faster. Not in some hokey romantic way. She didn't know what it meant. She had to look away.

'It was so silly, I know, but she kept asking for one. Her friend had one like it. Not really. Not nearly as nice. I saw it in the window and just went in and bought it.' Helen had to pause to shift the build-up of emotion that she could feel coming. It passed and she went on: 'It was only when I left the shop that I remembered or realized. I was a year too late. See. Very silly.'

She reached into her bag and pulled out a small green box. She opened it up, parted the white tissue paper inside and revealed the bangle. The glimmering light of the lit candles on the side altar coruscated over the cobras and their eyes shone.

'Most people would think I'm mad but . . . here.' She took the bangle out of the box and held it out to Goose.

'I will give it back. I promise,' he said.

Helen smiled and nodded. 'I know you will.' Goose could tell she truly believed him and wasn't just humouring him. That made him feel happy. And with Helen's endorsement still ringing in his ears he reached out to take the bangle.

'STOP RIGHT THERE!'

Henry Taylor's voice bellowed through the chapel, taking everyone by surprise. They froze on the spot, turning only their heads towards the door where they saw Henry framed in the entrance. He strode forward, marching down the aisle towards them.

'What the hell is going on?' he demanded. 'I don't know what sob story this little yob has told you, Helen, but I guarantee one hundred per cent it's not true.'

Helen's mind raced to try to catch up. She frowned at her husband. Did he know this boy?

202

'Mr Taylor?' Goose's mind was reeling too. What was his probation officer doing here? Had he tracked him down? Goose remembered now that he had missed an appointment earlier. It had completely slipped his mind. Then Goose realized that Mr Taylor had called Helen by her name. He turned to her. 'How do you know Mr Taylor?'

'He's my husband,' Helen managed to say. Goose couldn't believe it. He turned to Henry. He had never realized after all this time. 'You're Milly's dad?' he said.

Fury flashed across Henry's face and he lurched towards Goose. 'Don't you ever say her name!'

Helen and Anthony stepped forward to protect Goose, but Henry pulled back. He didn't understand what was going on. He had spent half his day chasing around the city looking for this kid, which caused him to be late meeting his wife to visit their daughter's grave, and now here he was.

Henry turned to Helen. 'This is who I was supposed to be seeing this morning, except – surprise, surprise – he never showed.'

'I lost Mutt,' protested Goose. 'I had to get him back.'

'Now I demand to know what is going on here!' said Henry. He looked down and saw the bangle, which was still in Helen's hand. Henry held out his hand and clicked his fingers. 'Come on. Give that to me.'

Helen bristled with indignation. 'Henry, don't speak to me like a child,' she said through clenched teeth. 'Now maybe you do know . . .' She stopped as she realized she didn't know Goose's name.

'Goose,' said Goose.

'Maybe you do know Goose, but have you ever actually listened to what he has to say?'

'Helen, I talk to him all the time,' said Henry, trying to keep his composure.

'That's not what I asked,' said Helen. 'I'm sure you do talk to him, but have you ever listened to him?'

'I'm not having this conversation in front of this little toerag. Now please give me that.' Henry held out his hand for the bangle. He didn't know the relevance of it, but clearly it was integral to whatever was going on here.

Goose looked from Henry to Helen and could see she was struggling to know what to do. Goose panicked, thinking that the bangle was about to be taken away from him. He knew he would never get it from Mr Taylor so he jumped forward and snatched it from Helen's hand.

'I'm sorry,' he said, and with that he turned and ran. He jumped up and over the first few pews, stumbled as he landed, but was on his feet instantly and headed towards the door.

'Come back here!' barked Henry as he pushed past Helen in pursuit of Goose.

'Henry! Leave him be,' shouted Helen, but Henry wasn't listening.

*

Goose ripped open the tall doors and tore out of the chapel. He jumped down the two wide steps at the front and started running towards the angel gates.

Henry was right behind him and gaining. In much the same way that Helen would drink when the pain of losing Milly became too much, Henry would run. Sometimes he would run three, four times in the same day. He would always take the most punishing routes and push himself to his limit, to the point when he felt as if his feet were bleeding, his muscles were cramping and he was about to throw up. Then he would push himself further. He would keep going until his feet were bleeding and his muscles were cramping, until he was vomiting by the side of the road.

Henry caught up to Goose quickly and easily. The builders, now all at the top of the scaffolding, looked down at the drama unfolding below. They stopped what they were doing and watched as Henry grabbed Goose by his hood and yanked him back viciously.

Goose spun and lost both his footing and his hold on the bangle. He crumpled to the snow-covered ground and Henry fell with him. Goose struggled to get his head up and watched the flight of the bangle. It rotated through the air in a wide arc. Goose's gaze moved on and saw where it was heading: the roofers' bonfire.

'No!' Goose screamed, but there was nothing he could do except watch helplessly as the bangle plunged into the heart of the roaring fire, sending up an eruption of sparks.

Helen and Anthony emerged from the chapel and saw Henry wrestling with Goose on the ground.

'HENRY!' Helen's shrill cry distracted Henry's attention from Goose for half a second, but that was all that Goose needed. He twisted violently, causing Henry's hand that was holding tightly to Goose's hood to twist with him. Henry was forced to let go. Goose leaped up and started running. He ran straight to the bonfire and in the same instant everyone could see what he was about to do. 'Don't!' cried Helen.

'Goose, no!' said Anthony.

'NO!' shouted the builders from the roof. Goose could see the bangle. He thrust his left hand into the fire, wrapped it around the scalding metal and pulled it free all in one swift movement. He was already screaming as he drew his hand out. The bangle was searing the skin on the heel of his hand. Goose had no choice but to let go. The bangle flew out of his grasp and landed in a pile of snow, where it fizzed and steamed. Goose dropped to his knees and plunged his blistered hand into another mound of snow.

'Come here, you little . . . !' Henry scrambled up and was coming after Goose.

Goose threw himself out of Henry's path, rolled, snatched up the bangle and spun on to his feet. He ran again. Henry started after him, but Helen had caught up by now and got in his way. She put her hands on his chest.

'Henry! Stop it!' she commanded. 'Stop it now! He's just a child.'

Goose didn't look back as he ran. As he reached the angel gates he stumbled, his foot snagging a pothole, and he took a heavy tumble. He tried to stay upright but scraped a knee on the tarmac, ripping his jeans. He could feel gravel digging into a bloodied graze, but he ignored the pain and kept going. He ran out through the gates and dashed across the road. A car had to brake aggressively. The driver smashed his fist down on his horn.

'YOU STUPID LITTLE BRAT!' he screamed, but his words were muffled by the fact that his windows were all closed.

Goose didn't stop; he didn't look back. He just kept running, clutching the bangle tightly in his hand.

Back in the cemetery, Henry was purple-faced with anger. He was panting fiercely, more from rage than exertion. He turned on his wife.

'You don't . . . !' He couldn't even finish his sentence. His teeth were clenched tightly together. 'I have to deal with these people on a daily basis. They are scum!' And Henry actually spat in his wife's face as he sputtered out the last word.

Calmly Helen wiped her cheek and shook her head. ''Scum?'' she said. ''These people'? My God, Henry, have you always been like this? So full of bile? Or is this just since—'

Henry cut her off. 'Don't!' he warned.

Helen was shocked by the ferocity of his reaction, but it only riled her more. 'Don't what?' she said. 'Don't mention our daughter? Don't mention Milly? Milly! Milly! MILLY! *MILLY!*' she shouted in his face.

'I haven't got time for this,' said Henry, pulling out his BlackBerry. 'We'll talk about this at home.'

'No, I don't think we will,' said Helen.

Her sudden calm unnerved him. 'What's that supposed to mean?'

'It means there's nothing left to talk about. Or at least no point talking. We both know it's over.'

'Now?' growled Henry. 'This is when you want to do this? Now?'

Helen shook her head sadly. 'I don't want to do this at all. I don't want . . . to be here. I don't want to *have* to be here. I don't want Milly to be dead. I want the life we had before. That was wonderful and perfect. She was perfect. You were perfect. I want that life. Not this one.' Tears were streaming down her face. She wiped her eyes and took a deep breath.

Henry frowned. 'You're just being . . .' but he couldn't finish his sentence.

'Being what?' asked Helen. 'Emotional? You should try it some time.'

Henry couldn't look at her. He looked down at the phone in his hand, studying the buttons. 6-4-5-5-9. He wrote out Milly's name as he had all year long, finding it in signs and adverts or in clouds in the sky or even once in the oily film on the surface of a puddle after a heavy rainstorm. She was everywhere. More than anything in the world he wanted her to be alive.

Henry prided himself on being a pragmatist. He never tried punching above his own weight. As a child, dreams of being an astronaut were quickly pushed aside. He decided to strive for the best life he could *realistically* achieve. He married as well as he possibly could, actually a little better than he deserved. Maybe the one time he did punch above his weight was with Helen. And maybe working in Manchester's probationary services wasn't in the same league as NASA, but he had worked hard and risen to a position of some authority. He had had a beautiful, bright, funny, loving daughter and had considered himself a very lucky man. His life might not have been spectacular, but it made him happy.

He had lost his daughter and now he was about to lose his wife. He had been frozen with fear the day Milly drowned and had done nothing to save her. He hadn't jumped into the canal like Helen. He had been punishing himself for that all year. Now here he was faced with another moment of decision. What he did next would determine all of his tomorrows. He had lost his daughter and there was no bringing her back, but he could still hold on to his wife. His beautiful, caring wife whom he loved more now than the day he married her. All he had to do, he knew, was tell her. All he had to do was put the phone away and take her hand. They could go away together. Go to the other side of the world if necessary. They could rebuild what they had. They would never forget Milly, but they could move on together. It was all down to him.

'I haven't got time for this,' he said, and he turned away, dialling on his phone. He hated himself more with every button he pushed.


Helen watched Henry walking away from her. She studied the back of his head and his shoulders. She knew this would be the last time she saw him. She didn't feel as sad as she'd suspected she would. She would miss the feel of his hair the most. She loved his hair. It was the exact same colour as Milly's.

'Goodbye,' she said quietly to herself. It didn't feel like

a snap decision made in the heat of the moment. This was something that had been coming for a long time. Only today had brought something unexpected: clarity. She wasn't sure where it had come from. Maybe from Anthony and Goose, or maybe it was just getting past the awful one-year-anniversary milestone. Whatever it was, she understood that a new chapter of her life was about to begin. It was scary, but she felt energized by it. She wasn't sure where she would go or what she would do. There was a great big world out there and plenty of choices. However, there was one thing she had to do first.

She turned and walked towards Anthony, who stood by the flickering bonfire. The setting sun was behind him and the last dying rays shone down on him, making him look more otherworldly than ever.

'We should find Goose,' said Helen.

'We?'

Helen shrugged. 'I feel somehow responsible.'

Anthony nodded. He understood. 'I think I might know where he's going,' he said.

A thought occurred to Helen. 'Who are you?'

'That's a long story,' said Anthony. They turned and headed to the angel gates and the busy road beyond.

## 20

# NAN AND THE FUZZ

The sun dipped behind the buildings and the streetlights flickered to life as Goose sprinted through the streets. Most of the snow had turned to slush and the pavements were grey and wet. However, there was a chill in the air that held the promise of more snow to come. It was late afternoon on Christmas Eve and the roads were quiet. Most people were at home with their families by now. Goose could hear carol singing in the distance, carried on the breeze. He wasn't sure exactly where it was coming from. He could just make out enthusiastic snatches of 'Deck the Halls'.

'Deck the halls with boughs of holly, Fa la la la la, la la la la, 'Tis the season to be jolly . . .'

Goose didn't feel very jolly. He pushed on. His lungs

felt as if they had shrivelled to nothing and a great bony hand was reaching into his chest and squeezing them tightly so he couldn't get any more air in.

He took short cuts everywhere he could. He knew this city better than anyone. The most direct route to the old Indian lady's house from the cemetery meant Goose had to go past his own house. He didn't plan on going in, but as he ran past something made him stop. He couldn't explain what it was, but he felt an overwhelming need to check on his nan.

Goose ran through the front door. The house was quiet.

'Nan?' he called.

'Is that you, Goose dear?' He heard his nan's quavering voice coming from the kitchen. 'We're in here.'

Goose headed to the kitchen, and it was only as he was on the threshold, his hand reaching out for the door handle, about to enter, that Nan's use of the word 'we' registered with him. He had enough time to think, *What does she mean, 'we'?* but not enough time to stop himself opening the door. Goose entered, and instantly wanted to back up and run the other way. Nan was sitting at the kitchen table flanked by a PC on one side and a WPC on the other. The PC, Storbridge was his name, stood up as Goose clattered into the room. He was big and imposing. He had hands the size of frisbees.

'Richard,' he said, 'I'm PC Storbridge, this is WPC Havelock. Your probation officer called us. Why don't you come and sit down?' Storbridge's voice was thunderous even though he was speaking at a neutral level. Goose wondered what it would sound like when he shouted. *Would it rattle the plates? Could it bring the building crashing down?*

Goose ran quickly through his options. He had to get out of there. Surely the best thing to do would be to double back on himself, but Storbridge must have been able to tell what he was thinking because he said: 'Don't try running, son. You'll only make things worse. Sit down.'

Goose looked forlorn. His shoulders sagged and he moved towards the kitchen table. As he eased himself into a chair, PC Storbridge and WPC Havelock started to sit too. Then, at the very last moment, as the two police officers lowered their guard and their bottoms touched their chairs, Goose jumped up, spun on his heels and raced back out of the kitchen. Storbridge and Havelock scrambled to their feet and gave chase.

Goose had a healthy head start, but the front door slowed him down. The wood in the door was warped from the damp autumn and it would stick from time to time. Now was one of those times. It only held him up for a second or two, but it was enough. Storbridge and Havelock barrelled into the hallway just as Goose strained to yank the door open. As it started to swing back, Storbridge's massive hand reached out, thumped against the door above Goose's head and slammed it shut. Goose was trapped.

'That was a very silly thing to do,' said Storbridge. Goose said nothing. He turned around to face the two coppers and wondered if he could get past them and back into the kitchen. Unfortunately the hallway was far too narrow. Storbridge alone practically filled it.

'You go make sure the old girl's all right,' Storbridge said to Havelock. From the look on her face it didn't appear she enjoyed being ordered around by her colleague, but she nodded and headed back to the kitchen. Storbridge turned to Goose. 'Now, Steve McQueen, let's turn out your pockets.'

Goose frowned. 'Who's Steve McQueen?' he asked.

Storbridge shook his head indignantly. 'You kids today. You don't know you're born. Come on. Pockets.'

The last thing in the world Goose wanted to do was reveal what he had in his pockets, but he couldn't think of a way out. Slowly, reluctantly, he started to empty them.

In the kitchen, WPC Havelock closed the door behind her. She could see that Nan was looking distressed by the drama unfolding around her. Nan was still wearing her apron and she was twisting the material in her hands and muttering inaudibly to herself.

'Shall I make us a nice cup of tea?' said WPC Havelock.

215

'He's a good boy, he is,' said Nan, out loud but not necessarily to Havelock.

'I'm sure he is, Mrs Thornhill. Don't you worry yourself. We all just want what's best for you and Richard.'

'Goose,' said Nan quietly. 'He's called Goose.' Havelock nodded and busied herself making the tea. Nan closed her eyes. 'Goose,' she said again under her breath. 'Goose . . . Goose . . . Goose.' Her eyes popped open and there was something different about her. There was a clarity and a look of determination on her face where usually there was only benign indifference. Nan turned her head to look at WPC Havelock's back. Nan was doing something she rarely did these days. She was thinking. More than that, she was plotting.

In the hallway, Goose was going through his pockets, removing the contents and placing everything on to a small table that usually held the telephone, which PC Storbridge had removed and placed on the floor.

There was a collection of junk of the type that Goose and most other eleven-year-old boys tend to carry about with them: odds and sods that he had found and stuffed into his pockets without thinking. There were tissues, sweet wrappers, sticks, pen lids, scraps of paper, his mobile and a small ball of Blu-Tack covered in lint. Goose made a show of patting down all his pockets one final time to make extra sure that he hadn't missed anything. He felt something in an inner pocket of his jacket and had to root down deeply to get it. His fingers brushed against both lots of money Frank had given him and the bangle; those were three things he didn't want to have to try to explain to a policeman. He drew out his hand and held it open to reveal the glass eyeball that he had decided not to give to Frank earlier. It was stolen, but he felt confident that Storbridge wouldn't guess.

'That's everything?' asked Storbridge. Goose nodded. 'Good lad.' Storbridge seemed to believe him and Goose relaxed just a little. 'Now put your arms out.' Goose's face dropped. Clearly Storbridge didn't believe him. He was going to pat him down. What could Goose do?

'Why? That's everything right there,' said Goose, jabbing a finger at the pile on the table.

'I'm sure you don't mind if I check for myself. Now put your arms out.' Storbridge said this more forcefully, and Nan's prized commemorative plate of Prince Charles and Lady Di's wedding that was hanging on the wall next to him did indeed rattle in its holder a little.

Goose's mind was blank. He couldn't think of any way out of this predicament, so reluctantly he raised his arms out to his sides. Storbridge started at Goose's left wrist. He turned his hand over and saw the red welt on the heel of Goose's palm.

'That looks nasty. How'd you do that?' asked Storbridge.

Goose shrugged. 'Burned it.'

'Well, I can see that, Mister States-the-bloody-obvious. How did you burn it?'

'Accident,' said Goose.

Storbridge wanted to press it; he could tell there was more to the burn than Goose was letting on, but he decided to leave it for now. 'Well, we'll have it seen to presently,' was all he said, and then he continued his search.

He patted up Goose's left arm and down the right. Then he went back to his shoulders and patted down his sides. He stopped when he reached the pocket in Goose's jacket where the bangle and money were hidden. 'Looks like you missed something,' he said, and reached into the pocket. He took out the roll of cash Frank had given him before he went to see Noel and the hundred pounds he had given him that morning. That seemed such a long time ago now. The surprise on Storbridge's face was plain to see. 'Now that's a lot of money for a young lad like you. Lot of money for anyone. Care to tell me how you came by it?'

'A friend gave it me,' said Goose weakly.

'What generous friends you have,' said Storbridge, loading his voice with scepticism. 'This friend have a name?'

Goose didn't know what to say. He didn't want to get Frank into trouble so he just shook his head. Storbridge didn't force the issue. He resumed his search. He put his hand into the inside pocket again and brought out the bangle. He whistled appreciatively.

'Friend give you this too, did he?' Goose just shook his head. 'We're not idiots, son. We know you've got previous. Housebreaking's your thing, ain't that right? You ever stop to think about your nan in there? She's not a well woman.' Goose muttered something that Storbridge couldn't hear. 'What was that?' he asked.

'I stole the bangle, okay, but . . . I need it. I need to give it back.'

Storbridge laughed at that one. 'Ten out of ten for originality, boy. You can tell it to the magistrate.'

'No!' Goose shouted, louder than he had planned.


In the kitchen, WPC Havelock was pouring the tea when they heard Goose's raised voice. Both she and Nan looked up.

'Stay here, Mrs Thornhill,' she said to Nan. 'I'll be right back.' Havelock headed out into the hallway, closing the door behind her.


'Everything okay out here?' asked Havelock. Storbridge glanced at her quickly, then returned his focus to Goose.

'Yeah, I was just hearing how Raffles here has seen the error of his ways. Plans to return all the hooky gear

219

he's nicked.' Storbridge held up the bangle. Havelock chuckled.

Suddenly the kitchen door opened and Nan came out carrying the tea tray. Before either of the coppers could react, Nan had walked into the middle of the hall, positioning herself very deliberately between them and Goose. 'Anyone for Battenburg?' she asked gaily. Then she looked at Goose and made a minute gesture with her eyes, indicating that he should run.

Goose couldn't believe it. After a split second of hesitation, he overcame his surprise and leaped into action. He jumped up, snatched the bangle out of PC Storbridge's hand and was already sprinting towards the back door.

'Stop right there!' bellowed PC Storbridge. Nan shrieked with fright and threw the tray into the air. Instinctively Storbridge tried to catch it. The hot tea drenched him. 'Aaarrrggghhhh!' he cried in pain and fury.

Storbridge and Havelock scrambled after Goose. Nan made sure to get in their way to slow them down as long as she could. By the time the two police officers had made it past her, Goose was already out of the back door.

Goose held tightly to the bangle as he came racing out of the back gate of Nan's house into a rubbish-strewn alleyway. Orange-tinted sodium streetlights shone down, offering small pockets of illumination in the darkness. He turned left and sped up.

Moments later, Storbridge and Havelock emerged. They saw Goose disappearing around the corner. Storbridge took off after him, calling over his shoulder to his partner, 'Head him off at the Cross.'

Havelock understood and ran over to their squad car parked nearby. She jumped in and started reversing at speed back down the alley with the siren blaring.

Goose slid around an icy corner. He glanced over his shoulder and saw Storbridge coming after him. Goose cut left abruptly and headed across a housing estate.

Storbridge barked into his shoulder-mounted walkie-talkie: 'He's heading across Clinton Court. Get him at Michaels Street.'

'Roger that,' said Havelock over the radio.

Goose ran past some garages at the foot of a block of flats. He went up a flight of stone steps daubed with graffiti and through a covered walkway where a fluorescent strip light flickered and buzzed.

He came out the other side and ran across some open ground. A group of young hoodies were gathered on a climbing frame drinking cider. They saw Goose coming and started jeering at him. They didn't know who he was – they just liked to jeer. Then they saw Storbridge pursuing him and they went quiet, hiding the bottles.

'I saw that!' shouted Storbridge as he passed by.

Goose came up another set of steps on the far side of the estate, through a gate and out on to the street. He could hear the siren of Havelock's car approaching. It was going to be close.

He looked to his right and saw the squad car. He just managed to dash across the road ahead of it. Havelock had to slam on her brakes to avoid clipping him. Goose didn't stop. He shot down an alleyway.

Moments later, Storbridge came up the steps and across the road. He saw Havelock.

'GO ROUND! GO ROUND!' he shouted, waving his hand in the air, gesturing for Havelock to head round the block in order to cut Goose off. She put her foot down and sped away. Storbridge took off down the alleyway behind Goose.

The alleyway was long and narrow. The walls on either side were high and Goose could see that the tops were peppered with broken glass embedded in the concrete to stop anyone climbing over. He looked back. Storbridge was gaining on him.

Then he heard the siren again and to his dismay saw

222

the glow of the squad car's blue flashing lights before he saw the car. Havelock turned sharply into the mouth of the alleyway. There was nowhere for Goose to go: Havelock ahead, Storbridge coming up behind. He was on the verge of panicking. *What to do? What to do?*

Havelock skidded to a halt ten metres in front of Goose and squeezed out of the car. The alleyway was only just wide enough so she couldn't open the door fully. Goose looked back. Storbridge was almost on top of him. The car was in front of him and Havelock was edging around to grab him. He had one chance. He found a reserve of strength and increased his speed. Just as Havelock brushed past the headlights, Goose reached the car and leaped into the air, landing on the bonnet. He didn't stop. He ran up and over the car and down the other side. Havelock tried to grab him but missed. Storbridge made the same leap on to the bonnet but he was a big man and not designed for leaping. His foot slipped and he face-planted on to the windscreen. He rolled off the side of the car and became wedged between it and the wall, his feet sticking up in the air.

'GET ME OUT OF HERE!' he yelled to Havelock, who couldn't help but smile at her colleague's predicament. She looked over the car. Goose was nowhere to be seen.

# 21

# RETURNING TO THE
# SCENE OF THE CRIME

Anthony and Helen were walking along quiet, mostly empty streets. Whenever they came to an intersection Anthony would stop and look in all directions before choosing which way to go.

'Are you sure you know where you're going?' said Helen after they had been walking for nearly half an hour.

'I think so,' said Anthony. The houses in this part of town were small and terraced. Street after street of mostly identical buildings, and Anthony was looking for one house in particular. And, to make it harder, he wasn't entirely sure where it was. He sort of knew in a half-remembered, half-told-when-he-wasn't-really-listening-properly kind of way.

They stopped at a crossroads. Helen said nothing and just let Anthony take his time as he looked down each of the roads in turn. Finally he pointed left.

'This way,' he said. They walked along another road that looked much the same as the last six. Though, unlike some they had passed through, this one was well lit by street lamps. Evenly spaced cones of light shone down on the white ground, illuminating pockets of dancing swirls of snow.

Helen was starting to think they were wandering aimlessly when Anthony stopped. Helen didn't notice for several moments and walked on. When she realized Anthony was no longer next to her she looked back. He was standing outside one of the houses, staring at it. She walked back and stood next to him, gazing up at the house. It was the same as all the others apart from one very obvious difference: it had a bright orange front door, which they could see clearly thanks to a street lamp less than a metre away.

'This one,' said Anthony.

'Are you sure?' asked Helen.

'Definitely,' said Anthony with a resolute nod of his chin.

'Why are you sure?' asked Helen.

225

'Not sure.'

'Wait. You're not sure now?' asked Helen, confused.

'No. I mean I'm not sure why I'm sure, but I'm sure. It's this one.'

With that he stepped up and rang the doorbell. They heard it *bing-bong* inside and they waited. After a few moments they heard movement, someone approaching, and the door opened inwards. An elderly Indian lady poked her head out and spoke in a broad Mancunian accent tinged with just a hint of Gujerati. She was tall though a little stooped with age. She had short hair, silver peppered with some black, and wore a pair of browline glasses.

'Hello, yes?' said Lal.

'Remember me?' asked Anthony, smiling. Lal frowned as her eyesight adjusted to the change in light levels from indoors to outside. Then she saw who it was: the strange man from the bus stop. The man who had looked for her bangle in the drain.

'You! What are you doing here? How did you know where I live?' Then those questions were quickly forgotten as a new thought occurred to Lal. She gasped, choked with excitement, and stepped forward. 'Ha! My bangle? You've found it?'

'Sort of,' said Anthony.

'What does that mean? Have you got it?' asked Lal with urgency.

226

'No,' said Anthony, and he saw a look of gloom descend on Lal once again. 'But it's on its way.'

'I don't understand,' Lal said.

'The boy who stole it is bringing it back.'

Helen glanced at Anthony: impressed by his faith in Goose.

'Well, you'd better come in then,' said Lal, and she opened her door wider.

Helen and Anthony stepped inside, wiping their feet on the doormat, and looked around Lal's small living room. There were two armchairs; one high-backed and the other low, with rounded arms. They were both covered in the same red leather and faced an old chunky television set that must have been twenty years old. There was a little set of three stacking tables nestled between the two chairs. One of the chairs was covered in magazines, newspapers and books of Sudoku puzzles. This was Meher's chair.

Anthony crossed to the French windows and saw only the reflection of the room he was in. It was pitch black outside. 'Are there any lights?' he asked Lal. She nodded, reached behind the curtain and flicked a switch. Outside hundreds of small white lights blazed into life. It was a wondrous sight. The strings of fairy lights were arranged around the shrines and statues, creating the most extraordinary display. They looked like a bright, chaotic spider's web stretching around the whole garden.

'Put them in for Diwali,' said Lal. 'But they looked so good I left them up for Christmas.'

Anthony pushed down the handle and opened up the doors. He stepped outside and walked to the middle of the small garden, turning in a circle, taking in the snow-covered spectacle around him with a blissful smile on his face. It had started to snow again, lightly but getting heavier. Lal's garden hadn't been disturbed since the snowfall of the previous night apart from the tracks of a few animals, mostly birds and cats: the birds looking for food, the cats looking for birds. Goose's footprints from the previous night had been obliterated almost as soon as he had left.

'It's beautiful,' Anthony said to Lal.

'Thank you. I know,' said Lal, smirking a little. 'This is my little slice of heaven on earth.'

Somewhere in the distance a church clock started to chime the hour. Anthony stopped and tilted his head to listen. He nodded to himself.

'He's coming,' he said.

'Who? Goose?' asked Helen. 'How do you know?'

All Anthony could do was shrug. He had absolutely no idea how he knew, but he felt sure that Goose would be there any moment. The three of them stood and waited in silence. The clock stopped chiming. Still they waited. After a while they all started to feel a little silly, standing there in the snow, all shivering, their teeth chattering.

'Shall I put the kettle on?' said Lal.

'Ooh, yes, please,' said Helen.

'Why not?' said Anthony, and the three of them started back inside. 'I'm sure he'll turn up sooner or later,' he said.

Just as they were about to step inside, they heard a scrambling noise behind them. All three stopped and turned. They saw a hand reach up and over the high brick wall. A moment later, Goose pulled himself up into view. He scraped his burnt hand on the rough stone on top of the wall and stopped until the stinging passed. He looked down and saw Lal, Helen and Anthony watching him. No one said anything. Goose hauled himself up and over and dropped down into Lal's garden in much the same way he had done the previous night when he robbed her.

Instinctively Anthony and Helen moved aside, allowing Lal to pass between them. She stood on the edge of the lawn and looked at Goose. He felt terribly self-conscious, what with everyone staring at him, but he was so close to the end now. He took a deep breath and stepped forward. He crossed the snow-covered lawn towards Lal. As he did so, he reached into his pocket and pulled out the bangle.

'I really am very sorry,' he said, and held it out to her. A tear sprang from Lal's eye and she smiled beatifically as she gazed down at her bangle. Then she reached out and took it from Goose. She slipped it on to her wrist and savoured the familiar feeling of its weight.

'You've caused me a lot of worry,' said Lal, but there was no anger or recrimination in her voice. She was merely stating a fact. 'I hope you had a good reason for taking it.'

Goose considered his answer carefully and then shook his head. 'Not really.'

'At least you're honest.' She paused. 'Well, you know, for a thief.'

'Are you angry?' asked Goose.

'Very,' said Lal.

Goose was confused. She didn't seem very angry. He wondered if pointing that out might be a mistake, but he couldn't quite stop himself. 'You don't seem very angry,' he said.

'What have I got to be angry about? I've got my bangle back, haven't I?' The truth was that Lal had been angry and desperately sad all day, but none of that mattered now. Not now her precious bangle had been returned. Lal held up her arm, rotating it gently. A thousand tiny lights glittered over the bangle's polished surface, making it look truly magical. The cobras looked so lifelike that for a moment Goose half expected them to uncoil and hiss.

'What's the writing say?' asked Goose.

'It's Sanskrit,' said Lal. 'It's a quote about Shiva. Do you know who that is?' Goose shook his head. 'People always think he's the god of destruction, but he isn't. Shiva just

230

knows that sometimes you have to destroy to begin again. To make the world a better place.'

Goose's brow furrowed as he thought about that. He couldn't fathom what that might mean. A thought was knocking at the periphery of his mind. He didn't want to let it in so he concentrated on something else and cast his mind back to history lessons. Wars were destructive. They destroyed a lot of things. Did they make the world a better place? Maybe on a worldwide scale. Maybe the world was a better place because of the Second World War, which he had learned about at school. Nazis = bad. No Nazis = good. That seemed to be the gist of history with Mr O'Brien. But what about all the people who had died? Being destroyed wasn't good for them or the people they left behind.

He thought about Kieran Moss, who was in his year at school. They had been friends once – back when he'd had friends. Kieran's older brother, Graham, was in the army and went out to Afghanistan. The convoy he was in was attacked and Private Graham Moss was killed. He was nineteen years old. He was given a medal, which Kieran brought into school one day. Goose remembered thinking to himself: *What use is a soddin' medal?* Was a medal really a fair swap for a brother? He remembered Graham and his mates would let them play footie with them. He'd liked Graham. He knew he would rather have a brother who let him play football than a medal any day. Just like he'd rather have his mum and dad back than . . . There was that treacherous thought that had been trying to get in. It had found a way, snuck in through the back door when he wasn't looking. Now he was thinking about his mum and dad and he couldn't stop. They were destroyed. How was anything better now?

The emotion of the moment got to him and tears started to well up in Goose's eyes, but he refused to give in. He wouldn't cry. He rubbed his face vigorously. Blotting the tears.

'That's not true,' he said, shaking his head.

Lal shrugged and smiled patiently. 'Like most things in life, young man, it depends on your point of view.'

Still shaking his head, Goose said, 'World's not a better place without me mum and dad.'

Lal stopped to consider Goose's words. Of course, there was no way she could have known his story. No one had mentioned it. 'Oh, I'm sorry,' she said. She reached out but Goose pulled away. Being touched by anyone right now would be disastrous. He'd be bawling like a newborn and he knew it. He kept his mouth tightly shut, choking back the sobs that were building up in his throat, locking them away until they passed. He turned to Anthony.

'Now, where's Mutt?' Goose demanded. 'You said I'd get him back if I did the right thing.'

'Did I?' asked Anthony, thinking back. He couldn't recall

saying that, but of course that didn't mean anything. Goose thought about it too and he knew that's not what Anthony had promised. He, Goose, had come to that conclusion on his own and was loath to let go of it. The alternative was too horrible to contemplate, but contemplate it he did. He couldn't stop himself. His eyes hurt from forcing himself not to cry, his throat hurt for the same reason, and there was a pain in his chest as if someone was squeezing his heart. His legs felt weak, like they were about to give out from under him.

'He's not coming back, is he?' said Goose. 'There isn't any magic. You're just some nutter.'

Anthony shrugged. 'Maybe, but—'

'No. No "but",' said Goose, cutting him off. 'I'm going into care and dogs . . . they run away.' Goose couldn't keep the tears out of his voice any more. He fought hard not to give in, but it was no use. His eyes were red and his throat felt dry. It hurt to swallow. 'Or get knocked over.' Images of Mutt lying dead or worse, injured, bleeding and in pain, in a gutter somewhere flooded into Goose's mind's eye. He screwed his eyes up tightly to try to block them out, but it was no good. His mounting anger had kept them at bay, but now the dam had well and truly burst. 'He's all I had left,' Goose wailed. 'It's not fair. Why is everything being taken away from me?' He covered his face with his arms to muffle his sobs.

Helen stepped forward, the mother in her needing to comfort the child in front of her. Within seconds, thoughts of a new life filled her mind. She was a mother without a child, and here was a child without a mother. A child so much in need. As was she. She so desperately needed a child to love and care for. She had been a good mother. A loving mother. She had devoted so much of those six years that Milly had been alive to raising her daughter as well as anyone could: teaching her, loving her, protecting her. Of course she had failed in that last aspect and her failure had had terrible consequences, but that had been an accident. It was not her fault, she told herself, thinking back to what she had said to Goose in the chapel. She didn't fully believe it, but she told herself again: *it wasn't your fault. It wasn't your fault. Bad things happen to good people, and good things happen to bad people. There is no pattern, no rhyme or reason. It's just life, and you make of it what you will.*

She saw her future now: her future with Goose. No Henry. He was gone. Goose needed her.

'Goose . . .' She started to speak, was about to wrap her arms around him and comfort him, but Anthony held up a hand and stopped her. That one simple gesture brought her plans crashing down around her. It wasn't lost on her how ridiculously easy it was for him to stop her in her tracks. And, as if a back door in her head had sprung open, the thought came that although Goose could be a replacement

234

for her own lost girl, what she really, truly wanted was to have her daughter back. To have Milly back. She could be a good mother to Goose but not the one he really wanted, no more than he could ever be the child she truly wanted. That child was dead and buried and could not come back. Ever.

Helen turned away. She didn't want to be here any more. She wanted to run. It felt to her as if the walls of this tiny garden were closing in on her. She felt like screaming. She opened her mouth to say she was leaving, but no sound came out. She was frozen. She couldn't speak. She couldn't move.


'Hold out your hand,' said Anthony to Goose. 'Where you burned it. Hold it out.'

'Why?' asked Goose.

'Because I've realized something. Something extraordinary has happened. Because I remember, you see.'

'Remember? Remember what?' said Goose quietly.

'Everything. Everything I'd lost. It's come back. '

'What? When?'

'In the cemetery. When you burned your hand.' Goose looked at his palm. It was red and blistered. It throbbed. 'I remembered my name and how I got here and why I'm here.'

'Y-you've remembered your name?' said Goose. 'It's not Anthony then?'

Anthony shook his head. 'Told you I didn't feel like an Anthony.'

'So what is it?'

'Hold out your hand,' Anthony said again. Goose didn't move. Anthony could see he thought it was a trick. 'It's not a trick,' he said. 'Hold out your hand.' Still Goose didn't move. 'Goose.' Anthony spoke softly. 'Trust me.'

Goose couldn't see where this was going. His mind was a mess. For most of the day, or at least the last half, he had just focused on getting here and returning the bangle. He had convinced himself that everything would be all right then. He would get Mutt back. He hadn't let himself think about what would happen after that. Now he thought about it. He wouldn't be allowed to keep Mutt. Mutt would be taken away from him and he would be taken away from Nan. She would be locked up in some dreary home that he knew she would hate. He would . . . what? Go to some horrible foster family or a care home full of unpleasant angry kids who didn't want to be there any more than he did. He was already planning his escape. He'd lost the money Frank had given him, but he had some more at home. He wondered if that was still there. Had the police searched his room? The money, proceeds of crime, was not particularly well hidden. There'd been no need. He knew Nan wouldn't go looking for it. All he had to do was put it somewhere

where she wouldn't take it by accident. Like the time he had hidden three hundred pounds in his trainers, only to come home and discover Nan had given away all his left shoes. He had no idea what had been going through her muddled head, but she had collected the left one of all her pairs of shoes and all of Goose's and given them away. She couldn't remember who to. Now he hid his money, rolled up in a sock, in one of the hollow tubular legs of his bed. He was fairly confident that Nan wouldn't give his bed away.

So all he had to do was get home, get into his room and out again without the coppers catching him. He wasn't sure whether that was going to be possible. But then again, did he even want to go? Alone. Without Mutt, nothing mattered now. First his mum and dad, then his nan. Maybe not in body, but definitely in mind. All he had had left was Mutt and now he was gone too.

He looked at Anthony, who was still standing in front of him waiting for him to hold out his hand. Goose had truly wanted to believe that some sort of magic existed in the world and that this strange, odd, weird, bizarre man could give him back what he wanted most. His little Mutt. But he couldn't. Life's just not like that.

Goose let out a long, slow breath and reached out his left hand. Lal and Helen looked on as Goose turned it palm side up, exposing the welt of the burn. It was in a very distinctive crescent shape. And it was deep. Goose would have that scar for the rest of his life.

'So there it is,' said Goose with a heaviness to his voice. 'Now what?'

Anthony took a deep breath and slowly started to remove the glove from his left hand. He hadn't removed that glove all day. It was always the right he would take off. There was a reason for this. He felt self-conscious about his left hand. He finished removing the glove and held it out to Goose, palm up. Goose frowned as he saw what was on Anthony's hand.

A scar.

A scar like his. No, not like it. Identical. The two scars were the same. The only difference was that Anthony's was old. Years old. But it was in exactly the same place on his hand and exactly the same shape. *That doesn't make any sense*, thought Goose. *How can that be?* How could Anthony have exactly the same scar as him?

'I don't . . .' Goose's voice faltered for a moment but he found it again. 'I don't understand.'

Anthony smiled. 'You will,' he said, and with that he clamped his hand on to Goose's. As skin touched skin, both Anthony and Goose drew in a sharp breath. They felt as if they had been snatched up in a passing tornado. Everything was spinning wildly. Lal's garden quickly became a blur. It felt as if the g-forces were going to rip them limb from limb and turn them inside out. Then a black hole opened up beneath them and they were sucked down into nothingness.

## 22

# BACK TO BLACKPOOL AND THEN BACK AND BACK

The whirlwind disorientation segued into a world of noise and movement, lights of every colour and people: hundreds and hundreds of people. Whizzes, bangs and music filled the air. There were a dozen different tunes and songs coming from a dozen different directions, mixing together into a cacophonous porridge of sound. Goose found himself standing in the middle of a crowd. His dizziness passed and he looked about him but didn't recognize anyone. He was surrounded by happy-looking strangers. Families mostly. Fathers with children on their shoulders. Mothers pushing buggies. Kids eating toffee apples and balls of candyfloss bigger than

240

their heads. The air smelled of roasting chestnuts and cinnamon.

Goose squeezed his way through the crowds until he found a little open space. He hopped up on to a low wall to give himself a better view. Was he dreaming? How did he get here? He recognized where here was. He was in Blackpool, and he could tell from the special Christmas-themed illuminations, which were impressive though paled a little in comparison to Blackpool's regular illuminations (which were also on), that it was Christmastime. He had been here before. Two years ago at Christmas with his parents as a treat. He had loved it.

However, something was different, but he didn't know Blackpool well enough to pinpoint exactly what. It was more a feeling. He glanced up at the soaring buildings that lined the promenade. He couldn't remember so many being so very high. There were advertisements everywhere playing on massive video screens. They were for products Goose wasn't familiar with. He gazed up at one billboard directly above him. It was for something called the 'eyePhone' by Apple, which, as far as Goose could tell, was similar to a contact lens. Plus people's clothing looked odd. So many styles he had never seen before.

"Scuse me,' said Goose to a woman walking past. Her skin was blemish-free and she was slim and pretty. She ignored him and walked on. Goose watched her go, thinking she was rude. She must have heard him. Then he noticed something as he looked at the people around him. They were all slim, tall, healthy-looking. This wasn't the Blackpool he remembered. Junk food was being consumed everywhere, but there wasn't a single fatty to be seen.

A man walked past, tall, broad-shouldered, chiselled jaw. He looked up, directly at Goose, who was on the wall.

'Can you help me?' asked Goose, but the man looked right through him. Goose realized the pretty woman from before wasn't being rude. She couldn't see him. No one could see him. He decided he was definitely dreaming. Strange thing was, he couldn't remember going to bed. Last thing he remembered was being in the old Indian lady's garden. He had given the bangle back. Anthony had taken off his glove and showed him a scar on his hand that was identical to Goose's. Goose looked at his hand and the scar. It tingled and looked fresh. Not like Anthony's. That was the same shape but it was old. Their hands had touched. Goose could remember a feeling of exhilaration coursing through him. Making every inch of his body feel weightless. Like being on a ride at a fairground. Suddenly he realized what this was. This was one of Anthony's visions. Except it wasn't Anthony's. It was his. Frank hadn't reported seeing anything when Anthony touched him. Neither had Dr Clarence, or Helen in the chapel. So why was he seeing this? What was he seeing? Why was he in Blackpool of all places?

Just then, Goose became aware of a familiar voice as it penetrated his subconscious.

'How about you, little lady?' he heard it say. Goose looked around, following the sound of the voice. He saw a small crowd of people a short distance away. That's where the voice was coming from. He jumped down from the wall and followed the sound. 'Thank you very much. I shall look after her. Don't worry. Interesting fact: if Barbie was life-size she would be thirty-nine . . .' Goose pushed through the gathering of people and found himself looking at a street performer. He recognized him immediately. It was Anthony. Goose noticed how Anthony stood out from the people around him. He was scruffy and unshaven. He wasn't a glowing picture of health. He just looked like a normal person.

'Anthony,' called Goose, pleased to see him, but Anthony didn't respond. Goose realized he couldn't see him or hear him, just like everyone else.

Anthony was holding a Barbie doll he had borrowed from a little girl in the crowd. He continued:

'. . . twenty-three, thirty-three, stand seven-foot tall and have a neck twice the size of an average human's.'

Just then, a car honked its horn nearby. 'Most car horns honk in the key of F,' said Anthony. 'Sure you've always

243

wondered that.' The crowd chuckled. He had them eating out of the palm of his hand.

Goose saw a small scruffy dog sitting nearby and he gasped. For a moment he was sure it was Mutt. But then the moment passed and he could see it wasn't. He was very similar to Mutt, but his colouring was a little different. He sat near a large coat and bag. Goose realized it was Anthony's coat and bag and therefore it was Anthony's dog.

Anthony put the doll on a rug in the middle of his performance area. There were several objects already on the rug: a hat; a football (which was emblazoned with decals that read: 'Fifa World Cup New Zealand 2042') and a ladies' purse.

'Right, I need one more thing,' said Anthony, and he walked around the front of the crowd. He approached Goose, stopped and looked straight at him.

'How about you, young man?' he said. 'Got anything for me?'

'Anthony!' said Goose. 'You can see me?' Suddenly a hand holding a plastic bottle materialized out of Goose's chest. It scared the life out of him. He jumped and turned around to see a boy, a little younger than him, holding out a bottle of Coca-Cola. Anthony took it from him.

'Did you know that Coca-Cola would be green if they didn't add colouring to it?'

'Yeah, I did know that actually,' said Goose.

Anthony returned to the middle of his performance area and picked up all the objects he had gathered from the crowd. He lifted one leg and balanced the football on top of his foot. Then, holding everything else in one hand, he dug into his pocket and pulled out his cigarette lighter.

'Lighters were invented before matches. Not a lot of people know that. And the late, great Sir Lord Michael Caine never said that in any of his films.'

Anthony flicked the wheel of the lighter theatrically and a large flame roared to life. Then he started juggling with the hat and the lighter and the doll and the Coca-Cola bottle and the purse. After a few moments of his audience oohing and ahhing he kicked the football up into the air and it effortlessly joined his juggling objects. The audience clapped and cheered. What a show. Then it all went wrong.

Anthony lost his balance and with it his rhythm. The cigarette lighter bounced off the doll and instantly set it alight. Goose looked at the little girl, whose eyes grew wide with horror as she watched her doll burst into flames.

'Oh no! Oh no! Oh no!' shouted Anthony in a panic as he started flailing left and right, trying to keep everything in the air. The fire spread from the doll to each of the other objects in turn until all of them were ablaze. 'Oh God! Oh God! Oh God! Owwww! Owwww!'

Anthony started screaming as if he was being burned alive, and then with an almighty surge of strength he threw all of the objects up and away from him. They were all heading for the audience, who screamed and started to back away, but there was no time. And then, just as the objects were over their heads, they vanished with a puff, and glitter sprinkled over the crowd. It took them a few moments to realize this was all part of the act and they were not about to be engulfed in flames. They looked up at Anthony, who was grinning and brushing the dust off himself. The applause came thick and fast then. Even Goose clapped.

But not everyone was smiling. The little girl who had handed over her Barbie was close to tears. Her bottom lip was wobbling. Anthony looked at her and said, 'I owe you a doll.' He paused for effect. 'Look in your hood.' The little girl quickly reached behind her and rooted into the hood of her coat. She gasped as she pulled out her doll. It was completely unscathed. The other people who had lent him their possessions searched their pockets and bags and found their items. The applause was even greater.

Anthony pulled out a hat from his overcoat and held it out for donations. Most of the crowd started to drift away without putting their hands in their pockets. This was usually what happened. However, a few members of the audience dropped some cash in. Anthony thanked them as they told him how amazing he was. Gradually the crowd

246

dispersed until Anthony was left alone with his dog and Goose.

As Anthony gathered his things together it began to snow. He threw on his coat. It was heavy and dark blue. Different to the one Goose had seen him wearing before. He pulled up the collar and whistled to his dog. They set off home. Goose, having nowhere else to go, followed . . .

Suddenly everything changed. Goose was disorientated. A moment ago they had been up on the promenade, and now in the blink of an eye they were making their way through a shanty town. A cardboard city. Goose could still hear the roar of the sea, but he wasn't sure from which direction the sound was coming. He was aware that there were people all around them, but he couldn't see anyone. There were small fires burning in large catering-size tin cans and the shadows moved. Even though he was invisible, he sped up to keep close to Anthony.

Anthony found a quiet corner in an alcove and he and his dog settled down for the night. Goose stopped nearby and watched as Anthony rooted through his pockets. He pulled out a small tin of dog food and opened it up. His dog tucked in, wolfing it down. Anthony took out a packet of dry-roasted peanuts and started eating.

'You're homeless,' said Goose as the realization

247

dawned. Then something caught his eye: some graffiti art on a wall nearby. It was an angel with the head of a monkey. Just like Anthony had asked him and Frank about. This must be Anthony's place. Goose felt terribly sad for his friend.

Anthony finished his peanuts and the dog finished his tin. Anthony wrapped his coat around himself and closed his eyes. The dog curled up next to him.

Then a repetitive sound nearby caught Anthony's attention. He opened one eye and listened: *Clackclackclackclackclack*. After a few moments he worked out what it was: the sound of chattering teeth. Anthony looked around, following the sound to its source. He pulled back a piece of cardboard leaning up against the far wall, revealing a young guy, barely twenty years old. The guy backed up, scrambling, scared.

'I don't want no trouble,' he said.

'Good. Me neither,' said Anthony. The young guy was shivering violently and little wonder. It was freezing, and the jacket he had on was thin. It was maroon with yellow horizontal stripes and matching yellow trim. On the left breast pocket was a badge. The badge read: 'My name is Anthony. How can I help?' Goose recognized it at once and frowned curiously.

'First night?' Anthony asked. The young guy, the real Anthony, nodded.

'Lost me job today,' he said. 'Me mam threw me out. Said I was a waste of space just like me dad.'

Anthony stared at real Anthony. It was clear to see how bone-numbingly cold he was. Anthony considered what to do and then took off his heavy coat.

'Here,' he said, holding it out. 'Swap ya.'

Real Anthony didn't have to be told twice. Instantly he was on his feet. He pulled his thin jacket off and gave it to Anthony. He grabbed Anthony's coat and wrapped it around himself.

'Oh thank you,' he said. 'Thank you! Thank you! Thank you!' He could already feel the warmth soaking into his bones.

'Just for tonight, you understand,' said Anthony, pulling on the thin jacket. 'I want it back in the morning.'

Real Anthony nodded vigorously. 'Course,' he said.

'What's your name?' asked Anthony.

'Anthony,' replied real Anthony, nodding at the name badge on his jacket. Anthony looked at it and held out his hand.

'I'm Richard,' he said, and they shook hands.

Goose looked on. He still hadn't put all the pieces together. He was surprised to discover that the man he knew as Anthony had the same name as him.

Anthony, real Anthony and the dog all settled down for the night. As Anthony pulled the collar of the jacket shut

249

round his neck a chill wind rattled through the cardboard city. He shivered and tried to ignore it . . .

Then, just like that, it was morning, which took Goose by surprise. He looked around and realized they were somewhere underneath the Blackpool Tower. He could see it looming above them through gaps in the roof. He heard movement and turned to see real Anthony waking up.

Real Anthony sniffed. His face, particularly his nose, was like ice. He pulled Anthony's coat around his throat. The rest of him was fine. It took him a few moments to get his bearings and recall the events of the previous night. He looked over at Anthony and his dog. The dog woke up, stretched and yawned.

'Awright, boy,' said real Anthony, and reached out to scratch the dog behind his ear. The dog liked it. 'Hey, errr . . . Richard?' said real Anthony, tapping Anthony on the leg. 'Wake up, mate. It's morning.' Real Anthony rubbed his hands together vigorously and blew on them to warm them up. 'Bloody 'ell, it's cold!' He shivered. 'Don't know what I would've done without your coat. You're a gentleman.' Real Anthony turned to Anthony and noticed that he still hadn't stirred. 'Richard,' he said, and tapped Anthony on the shoulder. 'I got a little bit of money. Not much,' he said, rooting through his trousers pockets and bringing out a few coins. 'But enough to buy us breakfast.

My way of saying thank you.' Real Anthony looked over to Anthony, who still hadn't moved. Goose was looking too, wondering why Anthony wasn't moving. 'Mate? Mate,' said real Anthony more forcefully. As he stared at Anthony's back, he realized he wasn't moving at all. There was no gentle rise and fall associated with breathing. Real Anthony scrambled over to him. He saw that there was a blue tinge to Anthony's lips. 'Oh no.'

Goose came over. 'Oh no? What's "oh no" mean?' The dog started to paw at his master and whine miserably. Real Anthony turned Anthony over on to his back and put his ear to his chest. He listened intently for a heartbeat but there wasn't one to be found. Real Anthony leaned back and sighed. He looked down at the dog, who had stopped whining and now had his head and front paws propped up on Anthony's leg.

'I'm sorry,' Real Anthony said to the dog.

Goose stared at the scene playing out before him with a look of incredulity on his face. He shook his head. 'I don't understand. You can't be dead . . .'


And once again everything changed in an instant. Goose was in a back street somewhere in Manchester. He knew it was Manchester instinctively. He heard a commotion behind him and turned to see his Anthony running towards him. He was very much alive. In fact, he looked younger than Goose had ever seen him look. A good five, maybe even ten, years younger.

He raced past Goose, unable to see him. Ten seconds later two burly policemen came thundering after him. They too shot past Goose . . .

As Goose turned to follow them, he wasn't in the back street any more. He was in an office somewhere, in the dark.

Suddenly the light from a torch cut through the blackness and Goose saw Anthony crouched by the desk. He was jimmying a drawer open.

'Ha! You're a thief,' said Goose. 'Pot . . . kettle . . . whatever . . .'

Again everything changed in a flash. Goose was standing outside a dark and imposing redbrick building with two turreted towers at the front. This was H. M. Manchester Prison, also known as Strangeways.

The door opened and Anthony stepped out. He looked younger still. He tossed a hold-all over his shoulder and set off down the street . . .

Now Goose was sitting on the top bunk in a cramped prison cell. The cell door opened and Anthony walked in escorted by a guard.

'Welcome to your new home, Thornhill. Dial one for

room service.' The guard chuckled to himself. Goose was frowning.

'What did you call him?' asked Goose, but of course the guard didn't hear him and left. Now the pieces started to coalesce for Goose. His friend didn't just have the same first name as him but the same surname as well. His name was Richard Thornhill. Just like Goose. *How could that be? . . .*

Again everything changed. Goose was in a large bathroom looking at himself in a mirror. There was something institutional about the place. It was white-tiled and grubby. A row of ten washbasins stood between him and the mirrored wall. He realized that his own clothes had changed. He was wearing jeans and a white T-shirt.

There was movement behind him and two boys about his age appeared. They too were wearing white T-shirts and jeans. Like a uniform. Goose expected them to ignore his presence, but they didn't. They crowded him, one on either side, and they made eye contact in the mirror. It took Goose by surprise.

'You got a big mouth, Thornhill,' said the one on his left.

Goose frowned. 'You can see me?'

The two junior thugs smirked. 'Yeah,' said the one on the right. 'Guess your invisibility cloak ain't working, Goose.'

And in that moment, in that second before Goose took a beating, he finally understood: Anthony was him. He was Anthony. They were one and the same person. Always had been, since the first time they met in the park. These two thugs could see him because he was no longer an observer in this dream. This was his dream. This was his life. This was his future . . .

Before the first punch landed Goose was running down a shopping street. There was a man chasing him and a woman was screaming after him to stop. Goose looked down and saw he was carrying a handbag. He understood he had just stolen it . . .

Without warning, everything went dark. Light from a torch cut through the darkness. Goose looked through a pair of French windows. The torchlight landed on the arm of a chair where it glinted off Lal's cobra bangle.

Goose was in the room, standing over the bangle. He reached out and picked it up. He heard a noise coming from upstairs. He turned his head and looked back at the bangle. He remembered this moment like it was yesterday. Wait, it was yesterday.

Everything went black.

## 23

# LAST CHRISTMAS

Goose woke to the distant sound of a dog barking. It wasn't much of a bark. More of a yip. A yip that belonged to a small dog. A puppy. And not so distant. Actually . . . close. Very close. In his house close.

Goose pushed himself up on one elbow and listened. His wild, all-over-the-place hair stuck out all over the place. Goose frowned and looked around. This was wrong. This was his old bedroom. He thought he must still be dreaming, but everything was so vivid. He could feel the texture of his duvet between his fingers, and the room smelled exactly as he remembered.

He heard another yip and realized this was the day he first met Mutt, the day he lost his parents. He had dreamed about this day many, many times, but it had never felt quite so real before. The dream was always the same. He would wake up in his bed. Hearing Mutt yipping he would make his way downstairs, but as he pushed the door to the lounge open there would be nothing but blackness, emptiness reminding him how alone he truly was and he would wake up crying. He hated those dreams and this time he wasn't going to play ball. He turned over and put the pillow over his head to block out the sound. It didn't really work. As soon as everything was quiet and still, the yipping, albeit muffled, still penetrated the feather pillow.

Gradually Goose realized something was different. Usually the dream just happened around him. This time he was dictating events. Putting the pillow over his head – he had never done that before. This was lucid dreaming. Must be. He hadn't thought about that workshop he'd gone to for ages. He sat up. There was yet another yip from downstairs. He didn't want to get his hopes up, but maybe this time it would be different. If he was really controlling it, maybe he could open the lounge door and rather than be met with nothingness he would get to see his mum and dad one more time.

He made a decision. He was going to go for it. He leaped out of bed. Almost immediately he trod on a toy: a Lego model of Imperial AT-ST.

'OOWWW!' He fell back on the bed and rubbed the sole

of his foot. He looked down at his bedroom floor, which was strewn with pieces of Lego and other toys and he had an incredible wave of déjà vu wash over him. The dream had never been this detailed. And his foot really hurt.

He wanted to get downstairs. He tiptoed across to the door, avoiding the many toy-based hazards along the way, and hurried out into the hallway.

He went past his parents' bedroom. The door was open. The white quilt was turned down at both top corners and up at the bottom on the right, where his dad slept.

He continued downstairs. He reached the door to the lounge and stopped. This was almost the end. Usually he would push open the door and that would be that. He had had this exact same dream thirty, maybe even forty times in the last year. He hated this part, but he really believed that this time would be different. Truth be told, maybe he didn't believe it but he hoped it more than anything. He closed his eyes, took a deep breath and pushed open the door.

One.

Two.

Three.

Goose opened his eyes and almost burst out laughing with joy. There wasn't emptiness facing him. He saw his old living room and his mum, dad and nan standing in a line, trying to look innocent, just like they had that day a year before.

'Hello, Mum. Hello, Dad,' said Goose, stepping into the room.

'Awright there, Sir Gooseby?' said his dad. 'What are you doing up so early?' It was just as it had been. Goose was wearing the biggest grin of his life. He ran to them and threw his arms around them, hugging them tightly. *Please still be here when I open my eyes*, Goose thought to himself. *Please still be here.*

He opened his eyes and his mum, dad and nan were still very much there, but looking at him curiously.

'You all right, love?' asked his mum. 'You have a bad dream or something?'

'No,' said Goose. 'Good dream. Don't want it to end.' Just then there was another yip and Goose remembered Mutt. He would get to see his dog one more time as well. He dropped to the floor. 'Come here, Mutt,' he called, and the puppy scampered out from behind his parents and started to slobber all over him. Goose was crying.

'You got a name for him already then?' asked Dad, clearly surprised.

'Yeah, Mutt. He's called Mutt.'

'That's a nice name, dear,' said Nan. 'Is it me, or is it a bit dark in here?' Nan crossed to the lamp in the corner and turned it on. It was one of those energy-saving bulbs that comes on dim and takes several seconds to brighten. Goose frowned. A thought started to bloom in his mind. It took a moment to become real and he thought back to the lucid-dreaming workshop once again. *You can't turn on a light in a dream,* he thought. His mind raced. *What did that mean?* It meant this wasn't a dream. This was real. This was last Christmas. He looked up at his parents and his nan. 'I'm not dreaming, am I?'

They all smiled and shook their heads. 'Good present?' asked Dad.

'We were going to hide him till tomorrow,' explained his mum, 'but he doesn't seem to want to play along with that plan. Happy Christmas, sweetheart.'

Goose wasn't really listening. A billion thoughts were raging around his head. This was real! His dad crouched next to him and smiled. 'He's had all his shots. Wanna take him out?' Goose started to cry but with happiness. There was a massive smile plastered on his face. Paul and Linda looked on with concern.

'Are you okay, love?' asked Linda. Goose nodded. The grin on his face couldn't be contained. It was threatening to go all the way around to the back of his head and meet up.

'This is real!' he said again.

'So you want to take him out then?' said his dad.

'No!' said Goose abruptly. 'You've got to go to work.'

Paul shook his head. 'Not today I don't. I'm not on call.'

'Yeah, today,' Goose said firmly. 'You've got to.' Paul opened his mouth to speak again, but before he had a chance the phone rang. Linda went out in the hall to answer it.

'Paul,' she called, holding out the phone, 'it's the station. Jamie's broken a finger, had to go to A&E.' Paul looked apologetically at Goose.

Goose smiled bigger than ever. 'It's all right, Dad. We'll take him out later.' Paul strode out into the hallway and took the phone from his wife. As he was speaking Goose looked around and saw his dad's car keys sitting on the coffee table. He snatched them up just as Paul dashed back into the room.

'Goose, mate, have you seen my—' But before he had even finished the sentence Goose was holding out his car keys.

'Here you go.'

Paul took the keys from Goose, shocked at how well his son was taking his departure. He had been sure there would be sulking at the very least.

'Thanks,' said Paul, and with that he hurried away.

Goose crossed to the window and watched his father go. His mum came up behind him and put her hand through his hair. Goose closed his eyes and savoured the touch of her skin.

'Don't be upset, love. You know he didn't want to go.'

Goose turned to her, grinning like a fool. He shook his head. 'I'm not upset, Mum. He's going to save her.'

With that, he threw his arms around his mother's waist and hugged her tightly. 'I'm going to get dressed,' he said, and dashed out of the room, calling over his shoulder, 'Come on, Mutt.' The puppy jumped up and raced after his master.

Linda watched them go, frowning. 'Save who?' she said to herself.

Paul was driving his jeep. He turned on the radio and 'Wonderful Christmas Time' by Tom McRae was playing.

'Oh, haven't heard this for ages,' he said to himself and started to hum along, slightly out of time. He took a right turn, going a different way to the route Linda took. Paul and his Jeep were nowhere to be seen when Eric Cutty in his red LDV Convoy van fell asleep at the wheel and crashed. This time instead of crashing into Paul and Linda, Eric hit a tree. No one was hurt. Not even him. The van was a right-off, but he told the insurance that he swerved to miss a cat and they believed him. Four months later, Eric was able to buy himself a brand-new van.

The Mercedes fire-rescue truck skidded to a stop on the towpath and two firemen scrambled out: Paul and Frank. Paul was the lead and Frank his support. The gathered neighbours and general rubberneckers who had come to see the drama unfold watched as Paul stripped off

261

his helmet, boots and jacket and, swapping places with Henry, descended on to the cracking ice to try to save Milly.

'Morning, miss,' said Paul with a smile. 'This is scary, isn't it?' He made the word 'scary' sound bright and exciting, like 'scary' was a good thing. 'But don't you worry, I won't let anything happen to you.' Paul sounded so confident that his confidence infected Milly. She believed him and she nodded just a little.

Paul took a step towards her and the ice crackled as it broke up beneath him. He froze on the spot and quickly made a decision.

'Hmmm, I don't think this ice is going to hold. What about you?' Milly was suitably distracted by Paul's conversational tone. She shook her head, agreeing with his assessment of the ice but forgetting to be terrified by such a thought. 'That means the next bit's going to be a bit tricky. Do you trust me?'

Milly was breathing hard, but she looked into Paul's eyes and he made her feel strangely calm. She nodded.

'Frank?' called Paul.

Frank stepped up to the edge of the canal. Henry and Helen were whimpering with fear. 'I'm here,' called Frank.

'Ice isn't going to hold,' Paul explained. Helen let out an almost animalistic howl of distress when she heard this. Henry's legs gave out under him and he dropped to the ground. Paul ignored their histrionics and carried on. 'You're going to have to bring us up quickly.'

'Understood,' said Frank. 'Ready when you are.' And he hurried back to the winch controls on the front of the truck.

Paul looked at Milly. 'Ready, Milly?'

Milly was shaking with fear. The honest answer was she wasn't ready and never would be, but she jiggled her head in a vague approximation of an affirmative nod. It was the best she could manage.

'Good girl. We'll go on three, okay?'

'What do I have to do?' she asked in a tiny voice.

'You just stand right where you are and let me do the rest.' Milly nodded. Paul smiled. She was clearly terrified, but she wasn't complaining or crying. He liked this little girl. She had spirit. 'When I tell you, I want you to take a really big deep breath and hold it. Can you do that?'

'Yeah,' whispered Milly.

Paul smiled. 'Good girl. Ready?'

'Ready.'

'One,' said Paul.

'One,' repeated Milly.

'Two,' said Paul.

'Two,' said Milly.

'Deep breath.' Milly gulped down as much air as she could. 'Three!'

On three Paul leaped forward, sailing through the air, landed hard on the ice and grabbed Milly. The ice exploded around them and the pair of them vanished from view, plunging beneath the freezing water. Helen screamed and Henry covered his face, unable to watch. Frank kicked the winch into action. It seemed to wind in agonizingly slowly. It inched up from under the ice. Seconds felt like minutes. Helen was staring down at the shattered surface of the canal, gnawing at the knuckles on her right hand. It was the only thing stopping her from screaming. Then she saw something dark emerging. It was Paul's head. His black hair was peppered with splinters of ice. As his mouth broke the surface he guzzled air and let out a cry of protest against the freezing temperature below. He was shaking violently from the cold.

Helen craned her neck, looking for any sign of her precious daughter as Paul rose up from the water, but she couldn't see her. A wounded wailing noise was just starting to build up in her throat when, as Paul's body swivelled slightly, she saw he had Milly clutched in his arms and was holding on to her for dear life.

'Milly!' Helen shouted. The relief in her voice was all too apparent.

Henry opened his eyes for the first time in near enough a minute and rose up to catch a glimpse of his daughter. He was crying with elation.

Milly raised her head in order to take a huge breath. That quickly transformed into tears. She was coughing and sobbing with a mixture of fear, relief and a reaction to the cold.

The gathered crowd cheered in celebration.

Frank hoisted Paul and Milly up on to dry land, shut off the winch and quickly wrapped the pair of them in blankets. Helen and Henry gathered Milly up into their arms and rained kisses down on her.

'Thank you. Thank you so much,' said Helen to Paul. She was weeping with joy. Henry pumped Paul's and Frank's hands.

'How was it?' asked Frank with a grin.

'Bracing,' said Paul. 'You should give it a go.'

'No, thanks,' said Frank.

That night Goose went to sleep with his parents in their bedroom along the hall. It was the best night's sleep of his life.

The next day, Christmas Day, Frank was up early, opening presents with Jemma and Alice. Nat King Cole and Dean Martin took it in turns to sing Christmas songs on the stereo. There was a knock at the door. Frank went to answer it and was surprised to see Goose.

'Goose? What you doing here? And this must be Mutt,'

said Frank, looking down at the puppy sitting by Goose's feet at the end of a lead. Mutt jumped up, excited to meet someone new. He ran through Goose's legs, tangling him up in the lead as he tried to get to Frank. Frank gave him a good stroke. 'You want to come in?'

No, can't stop. Got a couple of errands to run,' said Goose. 'Just thought I'd let you know, I saw a thing on telly about *The Happy Prince.*'

'What's that?' said Frank, looking blank.

'You know, the book.'

'Oh yeah, course. Think I've got a copy somewhere. Used to read it to Jem when she was little.'

'Yeah, that's right. I saw it on your bookshelf once, I think. Anyway on the telly they said it was worth an absolute packet. Like forty grand or something.'

'Yeah? Probably not our one though,' said Frank.

Goose shrugged. 'Don't know. Looked just the same. You should go and get it valued. You never know.'

'Yeah, right, maybe I will. Sure you won't come in?'

Goose shook his head. 'Merry Christmas, Uncle Frank,' he said. And with that he and Mutt hurried away.

Frank closed the door and headed back into the lounge, where Nat King Cole was singing 'O Tannenbaum'.

'Who was that?' asked Alice.

'It was Goose,' said Frank, crossing to the bookcase and scanning the shelves.

'Is he not coming in?'

'Had some errands to run, he said.' Frank looked through all the books and couldn't see *The Happy Prince* anywhere, but his bookcase was deep and there were three rows of books to every shelf. He searched back and back and finally found it tucked away. 'How on earth did he ever see it there?' said Frank to himself.

'What's that?' asked Alice.

'It's what Goose came over for. Said he saw on telly that this is worth forty grand.'

'Bloody hell,' said Alice, coming over to look. 'We should get it valued.'

'Yeah, we should,' said Frank, but then he tossed the book aside, took his wife in his arms and kissed her passionately. She kissed him back. Jemma looked on, rolled her eyes and smiled.


Goose and Mutt ran along a street of large detached Victorian houses until they reached Dr Clarence's imposing gothic monstrosity. Goose slipped through the gate, ran up to the front door and pulled the knob. He heard the sound of the old bell clanging somewhere deep in the bowels of the house and after a few moments he heard someone shuffling towards the door. He saw Dr Clarence's suspicious, beady eye peer out through the grubby stained-glass window. The old man frowned when he saw Goose and Mutt on his doorstep. He unlocked the door and yanked it open, a deep scowl etched on his face.

'Who are you? What do you want?' he snapped.

Goose smiled. 'You don't know me, but I thought you might want to look under the floorboard directly in front of your fridge. Has a big, you know, circle-y thing in it.'

'Knot?' asked Dr Clarence.

'That's it,' said Goose. 'Looks like Queen Victoria.'

'Is this a joke?'

'No. No joke. Look under the floorboards and you'll find a letter.'

Dr Clarence had had enough. Clearly this was some sort of irritating prank. He leaned out and looked up and down the street, wondering where Goose's friends were. He knew someone must be watching nearby and sniggering.

'Grow up, you little tit!' snapped Dr Clarence. 'You come round here again and you'll regret it, boy.'

Goose just smiled and started down the steps. 'The floorboard. Trust me. The letter's from your wife.'

Dr Clarence gasped involuntarily at the mention of his wife. He was about to lose his temper, but Goose turned and hurried away with Mutt scampering after him.

Dr Clarence slammed the door closed and stalked into his book-filled hallway. He looked ahead to the kitchen. For a few moments he contemplated what to do, then with a dismissive 'Pah!' he shook his head and went back into his study, slamming the door after him.

A minute passed and then another. The only sound was the *tick-tock-tick-tock* of the grandfather clock. Then the door to the study was wrenched open and Dr Clarence marched out, muttering angrily under his breath, annoyed with himself that he was falling for this childish nonsense.

He stomped into the kitchen and went straight to the fridge. He looked down and found the floorboard with the knot on it. It did look just like Queen Victoria. How strange he had never noticed that before.

He crossed to the drawer and took out his large flat-head screwdriver. Then, crouching down, he pushed the tip of the screwdriver through the crack in the floorboards and prised one up. Ancient nails protested as they were forced from their beds. Raising the board far enough to get his fingertips underneath, he then wrenched the board free and looked down into the cavity beneath. He saw the envelope, yellowed with age, addressed to 'Rafe', and once again Dr Clarence let out a tiny, strangled cry. He reached down and picked up the letter.

He put it on the table and sat down, staring at it. He would stare at it for the next nine minutes before he could bring himself to open it.

*

269

Goose took the long way home and passed by the house of Helen, Henry and Milly Taylor. He had made his dad tell him the whole of Milly's miraculous rescue over and over again until Paul had to actually refuse to repeat it any more and Goose's mum had to point out that his dad had had something of a hectic day and Goose should give him a rest. Goose pointed out that his dad had had an amazing day. He had saved a girl's life. Paul had to agree.

Now Goose needed to see them: the Taylors. He had to see Milly alive and well and the family happy to believe that it was all true.

Goose had tried to get the exact address out of his dad but, when his father wasn't forthcoming, he couldn't press the issue without raising suspicions. He did however glean that the house was just past the old lock.

Goose went to the canal and walked along. He found the hole in the ice. A neighbour of the Taylors, out walking his dog, was talking to some gore-hounds, who had come to see where the drama of the day before had unfolded. Goose eavesdropped as the neighbour pointed out which house belonged to the Taylors.

Goose walked around to the street side. The house was double-fronted with a semi-circular gravel drive. The curtains were open and, from the pavement, he could see a large plasma-screen TV playing in the lounge. He knew he had to be cautious. The crunch of the gravel underfoot could easily give him away.

He crept up to the window and peered in. He saw Henry, Helen and Milly all curled up together on an expansive L-shaped sofa, a bottle of port and two small glasses on the coffee table in front of them. They were watching *Scrooge* on their big TV. Alastair Sim's Ebenezer had just woken up after his momentous night and was giddy with delight at the prospect of Christmas.

The Taylors were oblivious to Goose's presence and, as he watched, Goose reflected on how he would never have to get to know Henry Taylor now. No more bi-weekly appointments. But now Henry wouldn't be as bitter and unpleasant as the man Goose had known. After all, Goose had met him shortly after his daughter had died, and as Goose watched them, saw Milly drifting off to sleep between her parents, and Helen and Henry exchanging a loving kiss, he realized that person would never exist.

Goose and Mutt ran all the way home in time for Christmas dinner. As he sat at the table pulling crackers with his mum, dad and nan and surreptitiously feeding Mutt little pieces of turkey, Goose thought about miracles. What an incredible place the world was. Magic existed. He was filled with a sense of excitement and wonder.

He thought about 'Anthony', which meant he was

thinking about himself. It was a mind-boggling concept to get his head around. He had actually met his future self. Except of course he hadn't. That Anthony – homeless-Anthony, street-performer-Anthony, walking-encyclopaedia-of-useless-trivia-Anthony – was a product of his parents' dying when he was just a kid. Goose looked around the table, watching his mum cut up Nan's food while his dad refilled the wine glasses. Hopefully that wasn't going to be a contributing factor in his life now.

However, the fact that this had all happened to him would be a contributing factor. He had changed. He didn't know how exactly, but how could it not have changed him? He had discovered that the world was more incredible, strange and unexpected than he could ever have imagined. He couldn't wait to see what the rest of his life had in store for him.

A thought occurred to him and he put down his knife and fork with a clatter, which caused everyone at the table to look up.

'Are you okay, love?' asked Mum.

'I just had a thought,' said Goose. 'What if you have to remember something for a really long time?'

'How long?' asked Dad.

'I don't know. Thirty years. Maybe more.'

'What would you have to remember for that long?' asked Mum.

'Well, don't ask me to remind ya.' Nan laughed.

'You wouldn't remember if he asked you to remind him in thirty minutes,' said Dad, eliciting a scowl from Mum.

'Remind him of what?' said Nan, looking blank for a moment before cracking a grin and dissolving into laughter. Mum and Dad started laughing too.

Paul noticed that Goose was looking very serious. Clearly his question was essential. 'Is this thing you've got to remember really important?' he asked.

Goose nodded. 'It is,' he said. 'It really is.'

'Then I suppose,' said Paul, 'you'll just remember.'

'Even for that long?'

'If it's important enough.'

Goose sank into his thoughts. It was important enough, and he knew he would remember.

## 24

# THIRTY-FOUR
YEARS LATER

Richard Thornhill drove north along Blackpool's famous promenade. He could see the illuminated tower in all its splendour in the distance ahead. He hadn't been back to Blackpool in twenty-odd years. Not since he had moved down south to seek his fortune, to find his place in the world.

Richard thought back to his childhood, growing up in Manchester. He thought back to the days when he was known as Goose. No one called him that now. Hadn't for decades. He'd gone from Goose to Richie then to Richard or Rich, depending on who was addressing him. But never Goose.

He wondered what the boy he used to be would think about the man he had become. He was an architect now. And a successful one at that. He owned his own business with offices in London and New York, splitting his time between the two cities.

Richard had enough money in the bank to retire tomorrow if he wanted to. He had a beautiful wife, Chloe, three children and three dogs. He glanced over to the back seat where one of his dogs was curled up asleep. Officially the dog was called Porridge. He had made a mental note never to let his children name any more pets. He, however, called him Mutt, and the dog seemed to like that more. He was, after all, the great-great-grandson of the dog Richard had had as a kid. That Mutt had lived a long and happy life.

Richard was forty-four years old, though he had lived one of those years twice ('the year that never was', he liked to call it) so in reality he was forty-five. However, he had never told anyone what had happened on Christmas Eve all those years ago. Actually that wasn't entirely true. Once, at university, at a party, he had got very drunk and told the whole story to a girl he was besotted with. She thought he was weird and never spoke to him again.

He had never told his parents. They'd retired a few years ago and now lived in the Lake District. After he'd done what he had to do tonight, he would drive there to spend Christmas with them. Chloe and the kids were there already, as was his little sister, Rebecca, her husband and their two children. Richard loved big family Christmases.

Earlier today he had stopped by the cemetery to visit his nan's grave. She had died when he was seventeen. Her Alzheimer's had been kept under control by his mother's loving care, and it never got as bad as it had been sometimes during the year that never was.

'In two hundred yards, turn left,' said the satnav. Richard pressed a button on the steering wheel and the navigation map was overlaid on the windscreen. He could see the turn marked up ahead. He let go of the button and the overlay vanished. 'Next left,' said the satnav. Richard indicated and rolled to a stop. Traffic was thin at this time of night. He only had to wait for one taxi to slide past and then he turned.

It was a narrow side street, barely wide enough for his car. A lot of old roads in the north were not suitable for modern-day cars. He drove to the end of the street and a dead end. The beach was ahead and an alleyway led off to the left.

Richard stopped the car and got out. Mutt/Porridge woke up and yawned. Richard opened the back door for him and he jumped down.

'Come on, Mutt,' said Richard. The dog obediently followed his master. They veered off from the alleyway into a cardboard city that Richard remembered well from his childhood even though he had only been here once. He was aware that there were people all around them, but he couldn't see anyone. There were small fires burning in large catering-size tin cans and the shadows moved. If his life had been different, this would have been his home. It had been his home but in a different life. One he didn't know.

Richard and Mutt moved deeper into the cardboard city, and the further he went the less memorable things became. He stopped and looked around, looking for some sort of landmark that would trigger a memory. Then he saw it: the angel with a monkey's head.

He moved towards the graffiti art and the shadowy alcove beyond. He stopped and listened. He had to filter out the distant roar of the sea and other sounds, but when he did he heard it: *clackclackclackclackclack*. He moved towards the sound and pulled the cardboard forward, revealing a young guy, barely twenty years old: real Anthony.

Real Anthony backed up, scrambling, scared. 'I don't want no trouble,' he said.

'Good. Me neither,' said Richard. The young guy was shivering violently in his thin maroon jacket with yellow horizontal stripes and matching yellow trim.

Thirty-four years ago Richard/Goose had made a mental note to come back to this place, at this time, on this day to find the person whose life he had once given up his own for. His dad had been right. He had never forgotten something that important.

'Hello, Anthony. My name's Richard. You won't remember me, but I remember you. What say you and I get out of this place? Got any plans for Christmas?'

READ ON FOR AN
EXCLUSIVE INTERVIEW WITH
EDDIE IZZARD . . .

EDDIE IZZARD *plays Anthony in the film version of* Lost Christmas. *Here he tells us about playing Anthony, and about his favourite Christmas movie and the people who inspire him* . . .

*What do you as an actor look for in a role?*
I look for a curious and drivable character in a good story, which sounds rather simple but it is the essence. And you have to train yourself to be able to know, or sense from reading, what is a good story and what makes a good character.

*What was it about the character of Anthony that attracted you to the part?*
I realized that as Anthony had no memory he also had no fear – which made him very ethereal to inhabit. I also decided that he had all the knowledge in the universe at his disposal, but he didn't quite know how to control it or when that information would appear in his brain. This combination made him quite a joy to play.

*Explain how you became Anthony – what's your process? How did you get into his mindset?*
For me to become someone, I have to bolt the intrinsic parts of their character on to the chassis of my own. With

Anthony I left my internal engine running on him but left him open – so he had a wistfulness but also a drive. He would just keep on going, affecting all the other characters in the film, until he felt he had finished his work.

*Do you have a dream part that you have yet to play?*
I don't have dream parts because I don't want to be disappointed if I don't ever get to play them. But I like playing physical roles with characters who have depths that you can explore. Having just played Long John Silver in *Treasure Island* and Anthony in *Lost Christmas*, I feel I am now being offered the roles I wanted to play when I started wanting to act - which was when I was seven.

*Who inspired you when you were young?*
Steve McQueen and Monty Python.

*Which person, living or dead, do you most admire and why?*
Nelson Mandela – he's shown what a great politician can do.

*What is your Mutt? In other words, is there anything that you couldn't bear to lose and would do everything in your power to get back?*
I already lost my mother, so nothing really compares.

*What are your favourite Christmas films?*
*Trading Places, It's a Wonderful Life* and *Lost Christmas*.

*Do you have any Izzard-family Christmas traditions?*
We used to write a list of what things we would like for

Christmas and then the list would go into the living-room fire and burn up and magically go off to Father Christmas.

*What would you have for Christmas dinner? Are you a traditional turkey man or do you go out of your way to avoid it?*
Always Turkey and all the extras.

*If there was a little Christmas magic in the world, what would your Christmas wish be?*
The gift of common sense, suddenly given to all the world.

## ACKNOWLEDGEMENTS

I would like to thank, first and foremost, John Hay, my co-writer on the screenplay that started all this. I don't know if it was your idea for someone to write the novelization, but thank you for stepping back and letting me do it my way. Even though we both know how much you love to 'tweak' my dialogue in the script. Thank you also to Eddie Izzard, who charmed the BBC, gave us the ending and stuck with us as we got the film going. Without the film there probably wouldn't have been a book. So thank you also to Sue Nott, Anne Gilchrist, Connal Orton and Elliot Jenkins. Thank you to Eugenie Furniss at William Morris Endeavor, who has held my hand as I've found my way into a whole new world of creative writing, and to Lucinda Prain at Casarotto-Ramsey, who has guided me through every avenue of my professional life for several years now and I hope will carry on doing so for many years to come. I would be rather lost without you. Thanks also to Claudia Webb at WME for all her invaluable help and hard work. Thank you to Roisin Heycock, Niamh Mulvey and everyone at Quercus. You guys do the best meetings and I could not be happier that you're publishing this. Thank you to Talya Baker for scrutinizing the manuscript so thoroughly and showing me how shockingly illiterate I really am. Thanks to Bill Nicholson for all your patient advice. Thank you to mum and David, who have always been supportive and encouraging and who have gone out of their way to help. I wouldn't have got anywhere without such great parents. Thanks to Carl McAdam, Jason Cramer, Vincent Holland, Julius Brinkworth, Toby Merrett and George Arton, because what's the point without great friends? And you lot are great! And last but by no means least, thank you to my amazing children, Joseph, Grace and Gabriel, Daddy loves you very much, to the world's greatest dog, Harper, and to my beautiful, wonderful wife, Lisa.